The Third King: Coronation
Brian D. Campbell

Printed in the United States of America
First Printing, 2018

ISBN 978-1-7329161-0-4 (Paperback)
ISBN 978-1-7329161-2-8 (ePub)
ISBN 978-1-7329161-1-1 (Mobi)

Red Cliff Press
PO Box 371
New Boston, NH 03070

Dedicated to Emily Campbell and Austin Campbell

The people achieving things in life you've always dreamed of accomplishing yourself are not all gifted or special. Most of them just ignored the voices that said they couldn't do it, especially their own.

Prologue

They approached with the morning mist, these three kings from parts unknown to any traveler. Each of them carried a gift for the newborn God-King, who was born that day into flesh to live a mortal life among man. The three kings were more god themselves than man, appearing like figures seen only in a dream. They moved about with no effort, appearing to never touch the ground beneath their feet. They seemed to glow as angels would, but they appeared to be men, though taller than any man ever seen, perhaps eight feet in height. They spoke no words, only gestured to the mother and then the same to the father as if asking for permission to inspect the God-King child. Once given the approval of the mother and the father, the three dream-kings each examined the God-King child. When it seemed the three kings were finished and satisfied they gestured silently to each other. They laid their gifts before the child and then the three dream-kings exited the manger and retreated the same way they came, appearing to float away and then vanish as the morning fog evaporates in the daytime sun.

Chapter 1

Most Thursday nights, Ben Gilsum could be found sitting alone, eating dinner and drinking draft beer at the bar of the Columbia Firehouse in the Old Town section of Alexandria. Old Town is the historic center of Alexandria and its boutiques, restaurants, antique shops, and theaters are a major draw for tourists. Old Town is one of many high-income suburbs of Washington, D.C. Not as modern in appearance as the business districts of DC, this small community also lacks the highbrow, overpriced restaurants and bars where you would find a typical young successful professional. Ben loved Alexandria because of its historic beauty and character, so he spent more time in Alexandria than he did in DC.

The Columbia Firehouse is a beautifully restored building built in the 1870s as the Columbia Steam Engine Fire Company. Ben's avid love of history meant this old building with its wood and brick interior quickly became his favorite stop on the way home from work. The Firehouse has the appearance of a pub when you enter the building. The 20-foot long mahogany-top bar that runs along the right side of the room has a row of heavy stools, each with a blue, leather-covered seat and back support. The building is kept impeccably clean on the inside and Ben enjoyed its charm and felt quite comfortable there. The restaurant is lacking any large waiting area, but patrons are greeted by a host at the door. As you walk past the long bar and a row of high-top seating and turn left you come to a beautiful dining room with exposed brick walls and high shaded-glass ceilings that allow in plenty of light. A row of elegant chandeliers hangs in the center of the room. The Firehouse is very popular in Alexandria.

Going to the Firehouse was an attempt by the extremely introverted Ben to boost his social activity and perhaps meet new people in his new neighborhood. Though Ben's crippling shy nature prevented him from accomplishing his original goal, he still enjoyed the atmosphere and continued to make the Firehouse a part of his routine. Most of the regular patrons at the Firehouse worked high-stress jobs in or around DC. And like Ben, a stop here allowed them to relax among friends and unwind with a drink before going home. Ben's need of routine and schedule meant he stopped here once a week on his way home from work and Thursdays suited him best. Ben drove to and from work most of the time, but occasionally he would take the Metro, the greater DC area rapid-rail transit system. There's a Metro stop at King Street along Ben's route home, and from there it's a short walk to the Firehouse which allowed Ben to enjoy a scenic walk along one of Alexandria's most popular tourist areas.

Ben was always warmly welcomed by the bartenders and wait staff because he was polite, quiet, and an excellent tipper. Upon entering the bar, the bartender greeted Ben with the usual, "Hello Ben, must be Thursday! How you doing, honey?" The staff often tried in vain to open Ben up with conversation.

"I'm good, how are you," was Ben's typical reply followed by a quick retreat to the nearest seat, saying little more. A petite waitress with red hair, green eyes, and a clear-fair complexion was always the first to approach Ben with her lovely smile to ask him what he'd like. She and the staff and regulars had become quite attracted to Ben, whose slim-athletic frame, just over six feet in height, was always a welcome sight. Ben was neatly groomed, with short dark hair and brown eyes, dressed in business-casual attire with expensive leather shoes, slim-fit suits, never a tie but sometimes a sweater or scarf over his fitted dress shirts. Though Ben's appearance of a sharply dressed, attractive, and successful young man would lead most to believe he was confident, Ben could never shake the inadequate feeling he developed as a child raised in poverty. This feeling kept Ben more than just a little humble and introverted and had stunted his social growth as a young man.

During those rare moments when Ben did speak, he was very well spoken, which helped to captivate his audience even further. Sadly, those moments were few and most of the people attracted to Ben at the bar had given up, speculating he was in a committed relationship or was a loner and simply not interested in anyone's company. But the pretty waitress with red hair persisted, never failing to pour affection on him and waiting on him whether or not he was in her section. And though her coworkers didn't understand why she continued her pursuit, she never gave up. She kept trying to win his favor even though the object of her affection would retreat any time activity or conversation were focused in his direction. Ben was often the subject of conversation after he left and was labeled a tough nut to crack. But she thought he was a nut worth cracking.

On weeknights in particular, the bar was occupied by the same group of regulars who had become familiar with one another. They were so comfortable, they often engaged in heated debates at the bar, prompting an occasional escort to the door by staff. They were typically back on their perch within a day or so, all was forgiven, and they were ready to begin a new debate. This particular Thursday the regulars were in full conversation about secret societies. Perhaps because the George Washington Masonic National Memorial stood high at the foot of King Street and the landmark dominated the visual landscape around Old Town. Their discussion ran the gamut. Why were the Masons typically only men? Were they run by billionaires hell bent on controlling the world? The consensus was that most of them were bored old men with lots of money who wanted to feel a sense of accomplishment and maybe even a sense of superiority while enjoying a night away from home in a fancy suit and funny hat.

One person in the middle of the banter caught Ben's attention above all others. She was a young woman with a thick Boston accent, he guessed barely twenty-one years old, who he had never seen before. It seemed to Ben that she was pulled into the conversation to defend her father and grandfather, who she said were Freemasons and Shriners. Most were familiar with both groups, but unaware of the connection between the two. The young woman from Boston said members of these societies were constantly giving time and money to charity. She explained to everyone how wonderful the Shriners Hospital was for children and how much of their services were no cost to the patient. She explained that her father had joined the Freemasons because he wanted to do something positive and beneficial for the world around him but never really knew how. The Freemasons proved to be a perfect place for him to figure it out. She mentioned a local group that no one had ever heard of, The Brothers of Herrad, which did amazing things in this very community, but admitted she didn't know anyone affiliated with that organization. Ben felt an immediate attraction to the young woman. Her passion, the soft feminine tone in her voice, and the youthful beauty of her face drew him in. Yet, he didn't join the conversation.

The patrons involved in the conversation, except for the woman who had Ben's attention, didn't care about anything they were saying. They had no real feeling about any of it. This was just another way to pass the time and make an otherwise boring night slightly more entertaining. Like most people in these situations, especially in places like a bar, they were barely in the moment at all. They were consumed with stopping to look at their phone to check messages or Facebook so their friends didn't lose sight of where they were or what they were doing. The Columbia Firehouse was a popular place to take selfies for social media friends to see. Some participants were looking at the silent basketball game playing on the TV bar. It was just another distraction that none of them had any passion for, but a nice escape from anything requiring any actual involvement.

This evening's debate was like all the others Ben had observed on Thursday nights. The fat man at the one end of the bar, with no one sitting on either side of him due to the lack of elbow room and his copious perspiration because he never removed his suit coat, would get red in the face, jowls jiggling, and would sweat even more when he got excited. The older, wealthy woman who always ordered a few too many bay breezes would argue back, but rarely offer a valid point. Ben paid close attention to the colorful discussions but almost never participated, often fighting the urge to shake his head. He usually ended up at the same place asking, *What are these fools arguing about now?*

Tonight's discussion was different. There was one person, the beautiful young woman with an endearing Boston accent who Ben had to force himself to stop staring at for fear of being caught, who was clearly different. Her accent bordered on grating. But her physical attributes were a lovely distraction from the actual sound of the words she was speaking. Her accent would be far more painful if her appearance wasn't as equally pleasing to the eyes. Somehow her beauty made it easier to forgive the fact she couldn't pronounce the letter *r* in any discernible way. Most of the words she spoke containing an *a* were stretched well beyond their required length and accompanied by an invading *h* or *y*, "Paaahk the caaah ovaaah theyaaah." She cared deeply about the topic and Ben was drawn to her because of that. Ben was just a couple years older than this woman. He was only two years out of college and in a new town with new surroundings, as he had recently started his job just a few miles north of Alexandria.

Ben left the bar without adding to the conversation and never trying to speak to the young woman who caught his eye. He went home alone as he always did, but the young woman and her passion stayed with him for the rest of the evening.

Chapter 2

Ben was quite successful for such a young man at just twenty-three years old; he was living well above any standard anyone in his family had ever enjoyed. Though he lived a comfortable life, Ben knew the sting of being poor. He was familiar with going without luxuries and sometimes without meals or decent clothes to wear. Ben spent the entire summer before eighth grade at Decatur Junior High School in Decatur, Arkansas, without a pair of shoes to wear. After three months of being barefoot, Ben was able to pull together two dollars to buy a used pair of shoes from a friend to wear on the first day of school. Though this and many other memories were a decade old now, they still affected Ben. He had yet to throw away a pair of old shoes since starting his career. His closet floor was covered with shoes he no longer wore. Poverty had also left Ben with a feeling of inadequacy that remained with him. He had a hard time feeling like he was good enough. The young man who grew up with less of everything than those around him had consequently developed a belief he somehow didn't deserve more and perhaps he wasn't worthy. This belief made it hard for Ben to accept a compliment, something that always made him uncomfortable.

Decatur, Arkansas, is located in the northwest corner of the state. It's home to a large processing plant that supplies mainly chicken and some other products to restaurants and retail outlets. The plant was where Ben's father worked for nearly forty years. Mr. Gilsum was a gentle, hard-working man with a strong work ethic and even stronger moral character. He had always been capable of so much more than he ever achieved but was distrustful of people in what he perceived as higher social classes. This misguided distrust kept him from ever trying to advance beyond a general laborer at the plant.

Unlike his father, Ben trusted everyone until they gave him a reason not to. He relied on his ability to read people to guide him. Though Ben had a remarkable gift for understanding people's intentions, his instincts weren't perfect. Sometimes, though rarely, he was proven wrong. This rarity got Ben into serious trouble when he was ten years old. Tommy Chadwin, an older boy who Ben admired and wanted to be friends with had stolen a litter of puppies from a mutual neighbor's backyard.

"Ben, buddy, look at all these cute puppies! The animal shelter wants me to sell 'em in front of Perry's Country Store for five bucks a piece. You wanna help me do it?"

Ben couldn't resist, "Awww look at them! Why do they wanna sell them Tommy? Don't they give puppies away?"

Tommy hesitated and answered with a crooked smile, "Well, yea, normally they do but they wanna raise money to buy food for all the other animals that don't have a home yet. If you help me sell these cute little guys, I'll bring all the money to the shelter."

Ben was excited to help his new friend Tommy, and the adorable puppy salesman proved to be impossible to deny. They were down to their last puppy when Ben solicited the rightful owner, who was horrified to learn the young men had sold all but one of her purebred Basset Hounds for five dollars each. Mr. Gilsum would remind Ben from that point forward of the puppy sale when he believed his son was being too trusting.

Ben shared his father's work ethic, but he admired his father's high moral standard above all his traits. Ben knew very few people who, when facing a situation that required a moral decision, could be counted on to do the right thing regardless of the difficulty or inconvenience it presented. His father was one of those rare people. The man never seemed to stray from his high ethical standards and Ben loved that about him most of all. The younger Gilsum would spend his entire life trying to live up to the same standards he had attributed to his father. It was a task he sometimes failed to achieve, not because he was an unethical man, but perhaps because he gave his father too much credit.

Like his son, Mr. Gilsum was socially awkward but he wasn't a shy man. Mr. Gilsum was gentle on the interior but rough on the exterior. He was a hard-working and weather-beaten man with little education but a great deal of common sense. Ben's grandfather died when his father was just a child and as a result Ben's father grew up in unspeakable poverty during a time when most people in the Decatur area were in the same condition. People avoided him because of his rough voice and appearance, but those who knew him considered him a kind, gentle, and generous man. He was not as polite or well-mannered as Ben, mainly because he was not raised by Ben's mother. Mr. Gilsum also had a hard time showing his affection or emotion of any kind toward those who needed it the most, like his son.

Mr. Gilsum loved his son dearly and often bragged about him to his friends at the plant. He wasn't a proud man, but he had a great deal of pride in his son. This pride and love could have gone a long way to help Ben develop his own self-confidence and perhaps even led to better social skills if Mr. Gilsum was more capable of showing what he felt. Still, Ben never held his father in ill will, nor did he ever complain about the lack of emotional involvement. Instead, he absorbed the same qualities.

A recruitment process by a private government contractor led Ben to the Washington, DC, area after four standout years at John Brown University in Arkansas as a dual math and history major. John Brown University was close to home, about fifteen miles south of Decatur. Ben's grades and near-perfect SAT scores enabled him to choose from a number of colleges across the country and combined with his financial standing, he was offered several scholarships. But Ben didn't want to be far from home. He was an only child and close to his mother, an elementary school teacher in Decatur.

Mrs. Gilsum was tall and full figured. She wore oversized, black-rimmed glasses for reading that often slid down her nose when she had them on, otherwise they hung by a silver eyeglass chain around her neck. She kept her dark hair short and neat. Like her husband, she was a lifetime resident of Decatur, but unlike him, she had a warm, receptive personality and seemed full of life and wisdom. Mrs. Gilsum was a favorite teacher at Decatur Elementary, adored by her students and their parents. She was well-known throughout town for her delicious peach cobbler and pleasant conversation. She was the only person Ben had ever known who understood him and all his quirks and oddities.

Mrs. Gilsum was diagnosed with muscular dystrophy soon after Ben was born. As he began elementary school her condition caused her to be in and out of work. Shortly after he entered junior high school she had regressed to a point where she could no longer work, but she remained active with the PTA and school fundraising, often contributing her famous peach cobbler for the cause.

Though Ben was gifted in his ability to read people's emotions, his own emotional attachment clouded his understanding of those close to him, especially people he loved dearly. Still, the times he felt truly at ease with himself were those times spent in his mother's company. Ben needed to be near her. He wasn't ready to move away and nearly stayed in Decatur after college but his mother wouldn't allow it. After watching her husband struggle for years at the plant with his own private guilt of the modest life he provided for them, she would not see her beloved son make the same mistake without at least trying to see what life could be like elsewhere. She knew Ben was special and capable of great things. She also knew there was little opportunity for great things in Decatur.

Given her condition, Ben's mother was tireless in raising her only child and teaching him to speak properly, conduct himself as a gentleman, and to always treat people with respect. Ben learned his strong work ethic from his father, but he learned how to be a good man from his mother. She never had to raise her voice or threaten any physical punishment to Ben as a child, not that she would ever bring herself to follow through with it. Ben always did as his mother instructed, as if he knew even at a young age the difference between right and wrong. Ben instinctively knew things even if he didn't understand why.

During his senior year at John Brown University, Ben was first contacted by recruiters from his current employer. They promised Ben that the work he would do would allow him to use the world's most advanced technology and that he would be doing his country a great service. He would be working with true patriots in our nation's capital and his work could take him to places all over the globe. Ben's mother knew of his potential and pushed him to let his talent to take him wherever it would go. And so, it took him to Washington, DC.

Chapter 3

B en was working as an intelligence analyst in an office just north of Alexandria. His company was a private business doing contract work for the Department of Defense and the FBI. Ben's role was to collect and analyze communication data for any potential threats or criminal activity, private or public, and report them to the program manager who would make final reports and send them to people with names like "Mr. Blue" or "Ms. Green." These were people sometimes heard on conference calls, but never seen. Ben never knew the results of his findings once they left his desk. He was also officially unaware of what tools were used to collect the data he was analyzing, who the people were in the communications, or if his efforts ever resulted in action of any kind. Working in this environment suited him. Ben was always an observer, often called a human sponge. He had a quiet but pleasant demeanor outside of work but never felt comfortable engaging in conversation, even with those familiar to him. He did however, pay close attention to everything that was happening around him and had what could be described as a photographic memory, if such a thing existed.

Ben had an uncanny ability to evaluate communications and determine if there was a threat or perhaps just a misunderstanding. He excelled at his job and the program manager offered him positions and advancement regularly. However, Ben had noticed the long hours and stress associated with those jobs and consistently turned them down. The people doing that work appeared to make close to the same salary but were clearly unhappy.

Theodore Seneca, or Ted to everyone who knew him, was a kind-hearted man who was just a few years from retirement. Ted was a couple inches taller than Ben, about six feet, three inches, with a broader build. The former all–American collegiate hockey player from Buffalo had a ring of short gray hair circling the large shiny dome on top of his mostly bald head. He wore a neatly trimmed, gray beard. Ted had worked for the company for thirty-eight years, starting as a cost accountant, working his way to controller, and eventually rising to the unlikely but final destination of program manager. He brought a much-needed practical sense to a group of techies who could build a PC from scratch but lacked the ability or perhaps just the aspiration to balance a spreadsheet. Ted had hired Ben, which at the time was a bit of a controversial decision.

A special recruitment process eventually brought Ben to Alexandria. The company used this process to find people that had all the required qualities you would expect to find on a typical outstanding resume or college transcript plus a few extra attributes that were harder for most private sector businesses to detect. Still, a kid fresh out of college with no military training or experience working indirectly for the government rarely started as an intelligence analyst at the company. The position normally required more than just a glowing resume or college transcript, even one scrutinized by the recruitment process. It required a security clearance. It required trust that if broken could ruin criminal investigations, embarrass the company, and eventually embarrass the government. People like Mr. Blue and Ms. Green did not like risk and did not trust new faces. They could not tolerate embarrassment. Ted said he knew right away that Ben Gilsum was not typical and after nearly forty years of being right about his hunches Ted's superiors knew that he was right. The company understood people like Ted and Ben had some sense about situations and people that most didn't. While most conventional businesses would dismiss things like gut or intuition and demand something more concrete to give them comfort over such a clear and immediate risk, the company believed Ted. So, they didn't question the hire.

Ben and Ted shared an instant bond. Like Ben, Ted could read people and their emotions and it was this ability that brought the two together. A successful recruitment led to an interview with Ted and to any outside observer, the entire interview consisted of a brief discussion about baseball. That was all Ted needed to deduce that Ben was genuine. Ted's hunch had nothing to do with baseball, of course. He instantly felt comfortable with Ben and when Ted felt comfortable with someone he trusted them. Trust was far more important than anything that any other recruitment candidate could offer. Trust and loyalty meant everything.

Ted also had a strong affection for Ben, which made Ben feel understood and welcome. For most of his life before meeting Ted, Ben was misunderstood. The connection helped Ben to excel right away. Ted trusted him and Ben knew it. They quickly became a hell of a team. Ted was a widower and father of seven. His youngest daughter was Ben's age and Ted often joked that if she hadn't married the son of a bitch she was hitched to now, he'd make sure she and Ben got to know one another. Ben was grateful for the son of a bitch because the prospect of dating the boss's daughter did not appeal to him even a little, no matter how much love he had for Ted.

Most of the work assigned to Ted and eventually to Ben was directed from the Department of Defense or the FBI through contacts within the federal government who acted as liaisons. It was common practice that employees at the company knew little about any of these contacts. Much of the communication to Ted and Ben came from conference calls or classified memos from people who called themselves colors, like Mr. Blue or Ms. Green. A great deal of the work Ben did was carried directly to the company by a man known as Mr. White. Mr. White was different from his counterparts. He came to the office more than anyone from the government and had allowed himself to be more involved with Ted and Ben than his superiors would have liked. The protocol for contact between the government and the company was that it was short, non-personal, and only as needed to do the job. Mr. White often broke that protocol and had become friendly with Ted, but then everyone was friendly with Ted. It was easy.

Ben was uncomfortable around Mr. White, not just because of this lack of following standard protocol, but also because the man gave him the creeps. He showed an unusual interest in Ben, often lingering around his office, stretching casual conversations longer than they should have gone on to a point of awkwardness. The younger man couldn't quite understand what his government contact wanted and sometimes wished he would go away. Mr. White was the only person from the government who ever spoke to Ben directly. He would often stop by Ben's office during his visits to the company asking how he was doing, if he was comfortable in DC, or how things were back home with his mother. Ben almost always felt Mr. White had an ulterior motive. There was just something disingenuous about the man but Ben couldn't quite figure it out. Ben thought it best to stay away from Mr. White as much as possible.

Mr. White appeared to be the same age as Ted, but Ben got the sense that Mr. White was nowhere near retirement. He seemed to enjoy his position with the federal government and the prestige it brought. Mr. White was always dressed in expensive, tailored suits, his gray hair slicked straight back with gel. Ben assumed this hairstyle was favored by men of power who had little time to fuss with grooming. It was a common look in DC. Ben often stared at a large gold ring that Mr. White wore with the letter M on the bezel. Mr. White knew Ben was curious about his ring, but he never acknowledged it. Ben always just assumed it was part of his flashy style.

When Ben started his career at the company, Mr. White approached him about someday working at the federal government under his direct supervision. That was if things went well at his current position, which they did.

Even then Ben felt uneasy and awkwardly answered, "I appreciate the consideration, sir, let's see how things go here. I promise I'll do my best to never let you down, sir." Unbeknownst to Ben, Mr. White often spoke to Ted about the same thing and Ted always told Mr. White that Ben was happy at the company, but would do a great job for the government, or anywhere for that matter. Ted knew Ben would never take a job working directly with Mr. White because he was well aware of Ben's feelings toward Mr. White. Ted was actually hoping he could convince Ben to take promotions within the company and perhaps one day take his role as he was preparing for retirement, but Ben consistently turned him down. Ben was happy doing what he was doing and he could tell the people in the jobs being offered to him were not. Over time, Ben also assured himself he would never work directly for Mr. White, but he was always cordial and respectful during their visits.

During one of many personal conversations between Ben and Ted that started about baseball, the conversation turned to focus on Mr. White. Something Ted said confirmed many of the uneasy feelings Ben was having. People like Ben and Ted never discussed the data they were analyzing or sending in report form to the government. They didn't receive questions after a report was presented and they were most certainly never asked for opinions.

"You know that bastard actually asked me a couple times what I thought about a submission," Ted admitted. "I think he may have even been trying to suggest I go a certain way on a report before I was done with it!" he continued.

"You ever consider talking to upper management about it?" Ben asked his boss and friend.

"I considered it," Ted answered, "But if you're gonna question the conduct of one of our government contacts you better have concrete evidence to support your suspicions. I don't have any proof and the brass around here doesn't give a shit about opinions. I thought it best to leave it alone."

Chapter 4

Growing up poor meant there was very little for Ben to do as a young child other than play pickup sports with kids nearby. These were spontaneous games of football, baseball, kickball, or whatever sport that was determined by the ball someone brought. The youth sport leagues in town required registration fees and equipment that Ben's family along with many other families in the neighborhood could never afford. When Ben arrived in the DC area as a young man, he didn't see much of this activity among the neighborhood kids. This motivated him to spend much of his free time volunteering at the Dunbar Alexandria-Olympic Club, which was a Boys and Girls Club in Alexandria only a few blocks away from the Columbia Firehouse. What started as an hour or two during large scheduled activities to help out at the club had eventually led to regular sessions where Ben would play kickball, softball, or flag football with a handful of kids. It was as if Ben had become some sort of volunteer Phys. Ed teacher. Ben loved volunteering at the club and it helped ease the homesickness he was feeling. Ben spent most of his time around DC in high-end areas with high-end people. He never felt quite at home in those settings. Spending time with kids at the club was an excellent way to relieve the increasing depression he was feeling about being away from home.

Ben had entered junior high school as a fairly decent athlete back in Decatur, playing football and running track. But his true strength was as an academic standout. When Ben turned 16 during his junior year he chose to give up sports to work part-time. Teenage vanity made going to school in worn-out and often ill-fitting clothes too much for Ben to bear. The only way Ben was going to get new clothes was to buy them himself.

One of his happiest athletic memories during high school occurred during Phys. Ed class freshman year. The class was made up of an almost equal quantity of seniors and freshmen, which was an excellent recipe for torment and pain for the younger boys. The class was playing softball and the insensible teacher allowed the senior boys to pick teams to play a game. The seniors seized the moment to form a team of bigger, older, and stronger kids to inflict further punishment on the younger, weaker, less-athletic kids in the class. Ben was appointed to the unenviable position of captain of the weaker team. Just before the start of the game, the boys huddled together to determine which positions they would play and exchange sighs and groans about how much this was going to suck. Feeling their anguish along with his own, Ben gave a speech to his team that inspired them to play like champions. The team of misfits and half-pints rallied and gave the seniors a beating. The freshmen who had been labeled "easy outs" by the seniors hit balls over their heads in the outfield. Kids who could barely catch were turning double plays in the infield. The group of undersized freshmen were playing ball with all the confidence they would have in a game among their own friends. Ben's words were enough to relieve the pressure and anguish of a kid about to receive a pounding from a bigger and stronger bully.

The energy during and after the game was something Ben would never forget. Some boys retold the story throughout all four years of high school. Ben would often think of that day with his fellow freshmen at Decatur High School as a source of encouragement when he was coaching kids at the club and things weren't going well. Ben's love of sports and his passion for helping kids with disadvantages reach their full potential inspired him to come completely out of his shell at the club. He was energetic, outgoing, and funny. The kids enjoyed being with Ben and games with him had become popular.

Ben enjoyed his volunteer work at the club and was proud of the impact he was making there. But he had also been inspired weeks earlier by the beautiful girl at the Columbia Firehouse and her explanation of why her father had become a Freemason.

"He wanted to do more for the community around him but didn't really know how," she explained. Those words stuck with Ben and made him wonder if he could do more. Ben didn't feel as though Freemasonry was a particular fit for him, mostly because of his perception of a bunch of wealthy old white men meeting in a lodge and feeling overly grand about themselves. In his mind, it was people like Mr. White who became Freemasons and Ben could not see himself in a fraternal environment with Mr. White.

There was another option, however. At the club, Ben noticed a group of men who called themselves the Brothers of Herrad who had on more than one occasion donated their time to volunteer at events. It occurred to him later that the beautiful girl from the Firehouse also mentioned the group as a local example of a secret society doing well for the community. The Brothers of Herrad also funded, staffed, and coordinated a series of pancake breakfasts at the club and open to the public to raise much-needed money for repairs to the building. In just a few such breakfasts, the funds provided by the men were more than sufficient and the repairs to the building were completed in short order. Ben remembered hearing jokes about how those must have been some damn good pancakes, because the money raised seemed far more than any of the regular employees and volunteers at the club thought possible. The Brothers who volunteered at the club always remained anonymous, only referring to themselves as Brothers of Herrad.

There was another time the Brothers had come to Ben's attention. Several months earlier Mr. White had directed Ben to analyze communication from the organization, but it proved to be innocent according to Ben's report. Ben remembered admiring what the organization was doing based on those communications and wondered why he had never heard of them before. Lately, it seemed he was hearing more about the secret society. *I really gotta look into this group a little more. This could be exactly what I'm looking for. Maybe they're accepting new members.*

Chapter 5

Ben was a person who labored intensely over important decisions in life. He had to think about his choice from all possible outcomes and he had to research everything he could find on the topic he was contemplating. It was the same for just about anything that interested Ben. He had to read about it. He had to pick it up, feel it, smell it, taste it, and turn it about in his mind. Ben could never ignore the desire he felt to learn more about a topic that caught his attention.

Nearing the end of the school year in sixth grade social studies class back in Decatur, Ben's favorite class, he brought up a problem he noticed to his teacher. There was something that troubled him. The rest of the kids in his class and the entire school were busy counting down the hours when they could ditch school for the summer. But something was distracting Ben. The textbook chapters each included a separate region of the world. The class studied each chapter in no particular order and was given quizzes and tests as they completed a region. Near the end of the year, Ben noticed the class skipped the chapter on Africa and he realized there would be no time to complete the chapter.

Ben asked his teacher during the last week of school, "Mrs. MacDougal, why are we not reading about Africa?"

"Ben, isn't it obvious," Mrs. MacDougal replied.

No, it was not obvious, not to eleven-year-old Ben. Eleven-year-old Ben was enjoying learning about all the regions of the world. How could he learn about the world with such an enormous portion left off the lesson plan? Her response puzzled Ben, and he was determined to complete the lesson on his own. That day the students turned in their textbooks for the summer, leaving stacks of social studies books from each class at the back of the room. Before heading to the bus to go home, Ben snuck into the empty classroom to borrow a book. Ben read about Africa on his own during the summer and returned the book on the first day of school the following year. Several years later Ben realized Mrs. MacDougal was concerned about racial tensions and she was worried about distractions a discussion about race could bring to her classroom. Even as a child, Ben became frustrated by not consuming all the knowledge about a topic he was interested in. He had to finish.

The first thing Ben had to do to make a satisfactory decision about joining a fraternal organization like the Brothers of Herrad was to consume all available material about them. For an introvert like Ben, the internet was the obvious source for what would be an extensive search at home that would go late into the night. Or so he expected. However, Ben could not find any credible information on the Brothers. There were only brief mentions about them from sources Ben learned at work and found them to be mostly false and conspiracy driven. Ben had an exceptional talent for knowing if what he was reading was true or manufactured. His activities at work highly tuned this talent and it caused him to believe everything he found on the internet about the Brothers of Herrad to be absolute fiction. But he knew the group existed so he continued his search.

After hours of not being able to satisfy his craving, Ben did some research on Herrad. Who or what was Herrad? All of his efforts lead him to one logical conclusion. Herrad of Landsberg was a French nun who lived in the 1100s. She was born in a castle in northeastern France in the historic Alsace region bordering Germany and Switzerland. As a young woman she entered a powerful abbey, the Hohenburg Abbey, which received support from the Holy Roman Emperor Frederick Barbarossa. Eventually, Herrad of Landsberg was elected abbess of the abbey. During her time, she became popular and loved by the nuns and throughout the community. The abbey was quite successful during her rule, becoming famous for its strict discipline and the great teachings of its nuns.

What made Herrad of Landsberg famous beyond her congenial nature was her work as an author. She was credited with creating the Hortus Deliciarum, *Garden of Delights*, which was a compendium of all twelfth century knowledge including poetry, illustrations, music, and texts by classical Arab writers. Perhaps the most celebrated feature of the work was the illustrations of various theosophical and literary themes. Hortus Deliciarum has been called an encyclopedia of the twelfth century, and it was the first such work written by a woman. The compendium was structured as a chronological presentation of Jesus Christ and the salvation of humanity. Images were strategically used in combination with text to deliver her message. There was a great deal of religious themes and scientific knowledge contained in the manuscript and it served as a tool to empower women inside and outside of communal living.

After spending much of the night reading text and staring at pictures created by someone who was apparently one of the world's earliest feminists, Ben felt he was no closer to understanding the Brothers of Herrad than when he set out to learn about them. Why were they so hard to research? He could find volumes about the Freemasons and spend weeks learning everything there was to know about them. But nothing about the Brothers. At least nothing he would trust to be factual. Ben gave up and went to bed, but his need for knowledge kept nagging at him and he couldn't sleep.

Ben's insomnia came mostly because he knew what he had to do to learn more about the Brothers and he wasn't at all comfortable doing it. Ben would have to use a more powerful tool to do his research. A tool only available to those with security clearance given by the government.

Though Ben had high moral standards and a deep respect for the rules at work and the law, he was convincing himself that a search into the Brothers of Herrad was harmless. Ben had a ferocious appetite for information which seemed to drive his decision and overpower his sense of duty. Often, Ben would just know something and not know why. In those cases, he found delight in confirming whatever it was that he assumed to be correct. Ben had a gift as well as a curse and this was one of those times this fact was going to lead him to bend the rules.

Chapter 6

It was a rare but not uncommon slow day at work. Ben struggled because he was exhausted from his moral battle at home the night before and also because one requirement of the job was to keep a log of his daily activity. Slow days made this troublesome for Ben because he would have to get creative about how he was spending his time. Ben liked being creative at work about as much as he liked bending the rules. He hated not having something to do but knew this free time would easily allow him to do what he needed to satisfy his craving for knowledge about the Brothers of Herrad.

During his efforts to fall asleep the night before Ben had come up with a plan to explain his actions if anyone asked him why he was using the software at work to research a secret society he had not been assigned to look into at that moment. Ben recalled receiving requests from Mr. White to analyze communications that involved the Brothers several months earlier. At the time, Ben didn't know why he was analyzing communication from the Brothers, which was often the case because knowing what you're looking for leads to bias and sometimes an opinion. And the government does not want opinions from a person like Ben. None of those communications had appeared to involve any criminal or even morally questionable activity. Ben remembered thinking what he read about the group during his assignment seemed to follow the same pattern he was seeing at the Boys and Girls Club in Alexandria. These were good people doing good deeds who had seemingly unlimited resources with which to do those good deeds. If anyone, specifically Ted, asked Ben why he was looking into the Brothers without an official open request, Ben would say he was following up on an old request from Mr. White. Ben was going to explain that he saw something away from work that made him want to check and be sure his old report to Mr. White was as accurate as possible. He would explain that after looking into the Brothers a second time, he was satisfied his prior report was, in fact, accurate. Case closed, again. Ted would almost certainly take Ben's word for it. The questions would stop and Ben would have the information he needed to make his final decision about the Brothers. The plan seemed simple. But Ben had still agonized over it all night, unable to sleep.

Using the same information he was given during his first assignment to review communications to and from the Brothers of Herrad, Ben was sure he could find more recent data. Still, what he found was the same seemingly innocent chatter about local charity events, donations to worthy causes, and discussions of topics at the next meeting of the local chapter. Had he been asked to review any of this again, Ben would quickly conclude there was nothing to suggest the group was doing anything unlawful. In fact, what Ben was reading only enforced what he thought before. These were authentic boy-scout types, doing good work in the community, and taking no reward for their efforts. Keeping their dealings private only added mystique, which was often enough for people to suspect wrongdoing. Sadly, suspicion was far too often all you needed to convince the public that someone was guilty. There are thousands of misleading publications about recognizable secret societies based on nothing but suspicion. Ben took pride in knowing he worked in an environment where suspicion and misleading publications were wholeheartedly ignored.

After reading the new information about the Brothers, he hadn't changed his opinion about the organization. *These guys are too good to be true! Can they really be this clean? What am I missing?* They were virtually unknown to the rest of the world and few pieces of any information about their existence could be seen by the public. There was something he discovered today that Ben could use to advance his desire to learn more about the group. This time he found an address. While discussing the agenda for the next local meeting, someone gave a location. *Holy shit! They're in Alexandria!*

Chapter 7

B en had escaped questions or suspicions at work about his use of company time and software to conduct the unauthorized search. *That's enough of that! What was I thinking?* He promised himself he would never attempt something like that again and in time, hopefully, the good that came from doing what he did would exceed the evils of misuse of company and U.S. Government resources. With his momentary lapse of principle behind him, he could relax and stop worrying about trying to cover his bad judgment with invented stories of following up on a closed matter. He could now focus on what he really wanted to do, find an avenue to use his time and energy helping others. Like the father of the beautiful girl he saw a few weeks earlier, Ben had always wanted to help but never really knew how. Hopefully, the Brothers of Herrad could show him a way to make a difference. And now that he knew where to find them perhaps he could get started. Now he needed to figure out how he would contact them.

After work, Ben drove his Jeep Wrangler to the address he'd unlawfully discovered to be the home of the Brothers. A brand new Jeep was Ben's first purchase after driving to Virginia in an old pickup truck he received as a college graduation gift from his parents. The old truck barely made it to DC and after his parents told him it was OK to trade it in for a better vehicle, Ben bought the car he always loved as a child and never dreamed he could afford. Driving his Jeep made Ben feel like he'd conquered poverty, though he still had plenty of emotional scars that needed healing.

The location Ben believed to be the headquarters of the Brothers of Herrad was on Duke Street in Alexandria. Upon arriving at what he thought was the correct spot, he found an unmarked building with no signs or symbols of any kind. Unlike most Freemason buildings he had seen, especially the visually stunning Freemason National Memorial in Alexandria known as the George Washington Masonic National Memorial, this building was plain. It was so plain, in fact, that Ben determined it was not a place that typically welcomed visitors of any kind. The address was for a unit in a large row house-style building, which are common throughout Alexandria. These buildings are typically two stories sometimes with an attic or short third floor. Though each unit shares the same outer shell with a common wall dividing them, the face of each unit is often different to create an image of separation. Sometimes brick row houses are painted a different color on the front with unique shutters. Often a different style or color of siding is used on the newer row-house buildings. There was no parking lot, only street parking, which is also typical in Old Town.

The building was dark on the inside and appeared to be empty. "Well, I guess that answers the question of how I will introduce myself to these guys," Ben said, talking to himself in his Jeep. "I'm outta here!" He decided it would be best to go home and write a letter to the Brothers and hope they would receive it and invite him to meet with them at a time he would be an expected and more welcome visitor. *Are they even around anymore? How come there's no one here? This doesn't make sense, I know this is the place.*

After agonizing over what to write Ben decided to keep it simple and to the point. The person reading his letter would not be expecting it, so

Ben decided they would prefer he keep it brief. If they wanted to know more about Ben the letter would provide several ways to contact him.

Dear Sir,

   I'm a twenty-three-year-old man living and working in the Alexandria area. I moved here only a couple years ago from Arkansas to begin my career after college. I enjoy the history and beauty of this place and spend much of my time exploring the area. I also spend a great deal of free time volunteering at the Boys and Girls Club in Alexandra.

   During my time there I witnessed the selflessness and dedication of several of your members to help fund renovations that ultimately kept the building from being shut down. This meant a great deal to the kids, to the community, and to me as well.

   I was hoping I could meet or talk with someone about membership with your organization. I have time to offer and want to do more for my new home.

Yours

Ben Gilsum

Ben signed and sealed the letter and mailed it the following morning on his way to the office after another night of tossing and turning over whether to send the letter at all. All the time he spent considering what to do and the confirming and reconfirming that this was a worthy organization gave Ben some comfort. But there was no such thing as an easy decision. He did nothing without a great deal of thought and deliberation. After only a few hours of sleep and a slow and painful morning, with the letter dropped into a sidewalk mailbox near a local strip mall, all that was left for Ben to do was wait and hope someone from the Brothers of Herrad would be in touch.

Chapter 8

I t was Saturday morning at the club and upon arrival, Ben was surprised by a quick visit from the Youth Sports Director. She was about a foot shorter than Ben and overweight. She had a significant waddle when she walked and both kids and volunteers at the Club referred to her affectionately as Duckie, which she didn't mind. Duckie had some particularly spectacular news to share with Ben. She was always upbeat and positive, so when she had good news to share she became animated and her eyes opened wide.

"Ben, we have a very exciting day planned," Duckie said with a radiant smile. "Better than we've ever seen!" she added. "We have a new volunteer who used to be a division one basketball player on board today to organize a basketball tournament and we need coaches. Welcome to the tournament, coach!" Ben tried to share Duckie's excitement but failed miserably. Basketball was never his game.

As Ben made his way to the men's locker room, he learned a few more things about the new volunteer. "So, where's the new guy, the D-I basketball star?" Ben asked another volunteer.

"Well she ain't in here, man!" the volunteer answered, laughing. *She?* Ben looked puzzled and his friend continued, "Are you kidding me Mr. Gilsum? You know the NCAA has *women's* D-I basketball too, right?"

Ben was embarrassed, "Of course, I guess I didn't think…"

Ben was interrupted, "Hey man, we're in the men's locker room. The perfect place to show your sexist nature, Ben. Don't sweat it bro, I did the same thing." Ben's friend continued, "Couple things you should know though. She's not from around here, has a funny accent. Thick Boston accent, I think. She's actually an incredible basketball player and she's super competitive. She's gonna kick our asses bro, even as a coach." Ben shook his head, he didn't care much about that. "One more thing my friend. She's hot, really hot, but you know what? Don't even worry about that man. Not like you're actually gonna talk to her anyway, Silent Bob!" Emphasizing the dig with a playful jab to Ben's shoulder.

Ben had never really liked basketball and had little knowledge of the fundamentals of the game. He had no idea how to coach it either, but he knew enough about how to motivate the kids and they usually responded well to him. Ben was a regular at the club and most of the kids that came to weekend activities there were quite fond of him. He opened up far more around the kids at the club than he typically did with adults. Ben enjoyed his time there, and it showed in the way he interacted with the children. He was a natural and the energy he felt knowing he was helping kids who grew up much like he did was both motivating and satisfying to him. He hoped that would be enough to go through the motions, get through the competition, and have some fun like he would if it were softball or flag football. *I know the basics; how hard could this actually be?*

Ben walked out to the back of the club where the basketball courts were full of bouncing basketballs and kids running in every direction after the balls and each other. He heard a loud whistle followed by a familiar female voice, a voice with a distinctly Boston accent he had heard several weeks before at the Columbia Firehouse. She was calling all the kids to order and motioning Ben to join a circle of coaches standing behind her.

"She remembers me," Ben thought as she gave him a warm smile and extended her hand to greet him. The smitten Ben Gilsum had been told the new volunteer was attractive, but he was positively stunned by his second encounter with Miss Angelina Rindge. The vision of the tall, athletic girl with long, wavy brown hair, bright blue eyes, and brilliant, provocative smile had stayed with him for weeks after seeing her at the bar. But seeing her again had jump-started his fading memory of her spectacular beauty. Ben was awestruck and speechless, his heart rate exploded and his nerves made him feel like a clumsy child. Suddenly, coaching kids to play basketball seemed like an amazing thing to do.

Angelina Rindge had recently arrived in the DC area to work as a personal assistant to a junior senator from Massachusetts. She graduated the prior spring with a degree in government from Dartmouth College and planned to attend law school while working in the area. Angelina came from a wealthy Boston family with powerful political ties that helped in her landing the job with a senator who happened to be a personal friend of her father. Despite her elite upbringing, Angelina was warm and pleasant to everyone she met regardless of social standing. She was outgoing, engaging, and delightful. In many ways, she was the polar opposite of Ben, which may have explained his helpless attraction to her. A person like Angelina could not only help Ben come out of his shell, she could smash his shell to bits.

"Hi, I'm Angelina, but my friends call me Angel. You here to help us get this thing going?"

Ben took a deep breath over a pounding heart. After what seemed like an eternal pause he managed to quietly murmur the words, "I'm Ben, nice to meet you."

His voice wasn't heard by anyone except Angelina and she gave him a wink, "I know your name, Ben. I saw you at the bar a few weeks ago. I've seen you there a few times. Patty told me your name." *Who the hell is Patty!? A few times?* Ben was puzzled. The terribly shy young man from Decatur didn't know the name of the waitress Angelina had interrogated for information, though he had seen her dozens of times. He said nothing, only offering a hopefully not too awkward smile in return. This had just turned into a very interesting Saturday.

Chapter 9

It was a lazy Sunday at home alone for Ben after what had turned out to be an eventful Saturday at the club. Ben rented a small apartment just west of Mount Vernon. He made his home in what was once the servant's quarters of a large and bustling single-family household in a secluded wooded area. Ben's apartment consisted of four rooms and a roof. There was a large bedroom, at least larger than Ben's bedroom growing up, with a good-sized closet on one side; the bedroom and closet had been two small bedrooms when the house was built. The other half of the building included a small bathroom next to an even smaller laundry room which was really a closet with a vertical-stacked washer and dryer. The larger open living room and kitchen space were separated by a small, two-person dining room table that Ben purchased at an antique shop the year before. These days the property was far quieter than in its heyday; it was owned by a widower who lived alone in the main house. He told Ben he didn't have the heart to sell the property after his children moved away and his wife passed. The widower landlord was quite handy in his day and had done an excellent job making the small apartment appealing. Ben fell in love with it the moment he saw it and the young man from Arkansas was an ideal tenant. He paid his rent without fail, kept things clean and neat, never made a sound, and had few visitors.

The main household was situated at the end of a long, horseshoe driveway, far away from the sparsely populated street. There were several tall, mature trees on the property that kept the house, and Ben's apartment, hidden from view to passersby. The unpaved driveway to Ben's apartment wasn't much more than a dirt path off the main driveway that ran to the left and rear of the house. It was bumpy, covered with large, overgrown roots from the trees all around, but Ben loved the solitude and his Jeep Wrangler had little trouble with the rustic path to his beloved home.

Ben kept up with most of the yard work, which was neither required nor expected of him. He also helped his landlord with any needed repairs around the property. For his efforts, Ben had a fantastic apartment in a picturesque wooded area which was only a few miles from George Washington's Mount Vernon Estate. An enthusiast of history, Ben was thrilled with the location, but it was the peace of the woods that made him truly love being there. Ben felt at ease in nature and the solitude of the woods was a must. Calm was a feeling he found impossible to achieve in a crowd. Being in the woods also helped with homesickness. Ben had grown up in the wide open and green spaces of northwestern Arkansas. In DC he felt claustrophobic, always surrounded by crowds and traffic. There was very little opportunity for a moment of peace and quiet. Having a place to escape to daily was a blessing.

As his Sunday afternoon drifted by on a cooler than normal March day, Ben found himself inside his apartment lying on the couch, feeling hopelessly infatuated, ignoring the television, and thinking about what happened at the club the day before. How a girl from Boston who happened to be named Angel showed up from what was hardly more than a pleasant daydream to drop the bomb that she had been asking about him. After she and her team of kids finished embarrassing the competition at the basketball tournament she had organized, she told Ben she would see him at the Firehouse some Thursday night real soon. This was a relief to Ben who was in agony trying to think of a way to ask for her number. Ben had a fair number of romantic relationships growing up, but they always started with the aid of friends or with girls he had known and felt comfortable enough to start a conversation. After moving to a town where he knew no one and had no close friends, Ben was experiencing a romantic drought. Attracting women was not the problem, but initiating conversation on his own was an impossible challenge for Ben. At last, it seemed there was someone who not only had his attention, she was fearless in breaking through Ben's shell.

Ben was busy rehearsing conversations with Angelina at the Firehouse in his mind when his phone rang, snapping him back into reality. He didn't receive many calls and before he pulled his cell phone out of his pocket, he paused and wondered if he had missed his weekly call home on Wednesday. He hadn't. Ben expected to see his father's name on the screen of his phone but instead it was an unknown local number. He decided to answer and was greeted by a youthful and proper sounding voice, "Hello Benjamin, my name is William Sullivan. I'm calling regarding the letter you sent to the Brothers of Herrad. I'm Senior Deacon and if you have a few moments, I'd like to talk with you about your letter."

Chapter 10

While Ben had been hoping to hear from the Brothers, a call from them so quickly stunned him a little and it took him a minute to speak, "Hello, Mr. Sullivan, yes, this is Ben. It's great to hear from you so quickly." Ben tried to gather himself and make the long pause seem less like he was wondering who the hell was on the phone.

"Excellent, Benjamin, do you have a moment to talk?" Billy Sullivan asked.

"Of course, Mr. Sullivan, but please call me Ben," Ben quickly answered.

Ben absolutely hated to be called Benjamin. It reminded him of childhood memories going to church with his aunt who felt it was her duty to take the boy to church every Sunday because her sister, Ben's mother, refused to force Ben to go as a child. Ben's parents weren't religious and their approach was to allow Ben to make up his own mind about church. He could go if he wanted to and they encouraged it, but they would never force him to go or to stay home. Ben always agreed to go with his aunt but not because he was curious about religion. They had free donuts and to Ben, a donut was a far better choice for breakfast on Sunday morning than a piece of toast with butter and a sprinkle of sugar if he was lucky.

He didn't mind the sermon and in fact, he enjoyed Bible stories very much. Ben disliked what happened when he first arrived at church. All the children were brought to a room where they played together, except for the shy and shabbily dressed Ben who would find a quiet place in the corner to read a book. The combination of his bashfulness and his shoddy clothes made it impossible for Ben to make friends. All the other kids were dressed in their Sunday best and they were content to ignore Ben.

Solitude and shame for his appearance were still not the worst part of going to church for the very young Ben. He had become accustomed to those things. What Ben found insufferable in the children's room was that the young women who were barely teenagers assigned to watch the kids would call him Benjamin David despite his repeated protests. The other children also called him Benjamin David because that's what the older girls called him and because they knew he didn't like it. Still, that was a small price to pay for a donut. As Ben got older he eventually gave up his Sundays at church but to this day he detested being called Benjamin. And he also came to loathe donuts.

"Very well, Ben, and please stop it with the 'Mr. Sullivan.' You can call me Billy." With that out of the way, the two young men talked for nearly an hour about their hometowns, where they went to college, what they were doing for work, their favorite sports, and which teams they rooted for. Many of Ben's fears that the Brothers of Herrad were another fraternal organization full of old men with nothing better to do were vanishing during their conversation. Ben was eager to hear more and to meet Billy if that was to come next. Billy, however, changed his tone when it came time to talk business and didn't seem ready to set up a meeting. Ben could sense a more robotic tone when the conversation shifted to the Brothers as if Billy were reading from a script. Ben didn't give it much concern, thinking perhaps the young man was new to his position of authority.

With his tone going back to serious, Billy asked Ben a question that was a bit difficult to answer. "Ben, I have to ask you a question. How did you find us? We're not the Freemasons. We don't advertise on television to men seeking to reach their full potential or to achieve the true greatness that may be inside you. Normally our members come to us because someone sent them here. Did someone reach out to you?"

Ben's sense of calm quickly turned to apprehension. When he discussed his work with Billy, he didn't mention he was an intelligence analyst or that he worked indirectly for the federal government. He said he worked as a project manager for a government contractor, which was not actually false, though misleading as to what he did at work. He would never have told Billy how he found the Brothers' contact information regardless, but now he had to think fast.

To avoid another long pause like at the beginning of their conversation, Ben talked quickly, "I do volunteer work at the Boys and Girls Club in Alexandria. A couple of your members come and help out a lot there. They even sponsored breakfasts to raise money to save the building." Realizing he hadn't yet explained how he got an address, Ben hoped if he talked at length about what the Brothers who volunteered were doing he could distract Billy from asking.

Billy could easily pick up on the nervousness in Ben's voice, so he interrupted him, "This is not a problem Ben, I was just curious. I'm quite impressed that you could get in touch with us without help from someone here. I'm not aware of that happening before." Ben could tell Billy wasn't satisfied with the non-answer and he was being polite by not pressing but Ben couldn't tell Billy the truth and he was happy to let it go at that.

Another uncomfortable pause followed because Ben wasn't going to say anything else until Billy asked a question or started a new topic. This was not uncommon for Ben during a conversation. It wasn't due to lack of interest or respect. Ben was fond of Billy already based on the last hour on the phone and he was hoping Billy would suggest they meet and talk more about the Brothers of Herrad. When a topic of conversation reached its natural end Ben tended to not know what to say. Ben was never very good at starting a conversation, even with people he was comfortable with.

As pause led to near panic for Ben, Billy finally let him off the hook and moved the conversation forward and at a quick, yet robotic pace. He wasted no time getting to the point and he was clear and thorough. For a person like Ben, who suffered immensely during small talk, this was greatly appreciated. "Ben, I have your address from the letter you sent us. The normal process for accepting new members begins with a visit from two people within our organization. They will have some prepared questions to ask you and your answers will determine the next step. Permission for you to seek initiation has to be requested by one of those members during one of our monthly assemblies and then seconded by the other. They will then share the information they gathered from you during their visit. If that request and second is accepted unanimously during the assembly, you will be contacted a second time by one of those members. That person will become your mentor through every part of your journey to become a member and beyond. Would you like me to arrange the visit?"

Ben thought about everything Billy had just told him. Though he wanted to meet with someone and talk more about the Brothers, this seemed like a step toward joining the group before he had time to follow his typical, lengthy, and painful decision-making process. Despite his reservations, Ben figured he would ask more questions during the visit and told Billy he would welcome the Brothers to his home for a meeting.

Chapter 11

B en was quietly sipping his IPA at the Firehouse on Thursday after finishing one of his favorite meals; a Firehouse burger and beer-battered onion rings with chipotle mayo. This was a treat for the normally calorie-conscious young man who anxiously stared at the entrance of the bar hoping and fearing at the same time that this was the night a now familiar Angelina Rindge would be "seeing him at the Firehouse." He'd imagined the encounter at least a hundred times and rehearsed at least a hundred different conversations leading up to this night. He was excited about meeting someone, which was a feeling he hadn't felt since moving to Alexandria. And now there were at least two forthcoming encounters that had his mind and heart racing with eagerness, one with Angelina and the other with the Brothers. Tonight, he recognized his anticipation and fear of the first encounter as Angelina appeared and headed for the barstool next to him. She was wearing a tight, sleeveless light-gray turtleneck which seemed inadequate for such a cool evening, but Ben wasn't complaining. She was stunning, with her typical striking and engaging smile. Ben's heart was pounding so hard it nearly hurt, but he managed a welcoming smile in return.

"Fancy meeting you here, handsome, I guess that means it's Thursday," Angelina beamed. *Handsome!?* All that Ben could muster was a smile. Angelina knew more about Ben than he realized. She knew he was shy, painfully, bashfully shy. She also knew he was kind-hearted, attractive, and polite. She assumed he was relatively successful based on his articulate speech when he actually spoke. She also picked up on the fact that he was living alone far from home in a relatively expensive area with enough money to dress in expensive, tasteful clothing and dine regularly at a trendy spot in Old Town. This information was apparently gathered by personal observation and by asking the bartenders and wait staff at the Firehouse questions about the object of her infatuation.

Angelina's personality was the opposite of Ben's. She was outgoing, never afraid to speak her mind, and invited a conversation with everyone she met. She had seen Ben at the Firehouse several weeks earlier and was immediately attracted to him. She questioned the staff and other patrons about Ben and quickly announced she would be the first to break his shell. She told them that after seeing Ben at the Boys and Girls Club she was determined to make her move before someone else did and made it clear to the other women at the bar, staff included, that she was going for it. The staff was, with one exception, excited at the idea of someone finally making a move on Ben and were ready to offer any support they could. The exception was the petite waitress with red hair who was devastated to have such tough and attractive competition for Ben's heart. Still, she wouldn't stand in Angelina's way, not that it would have slowed down the woman from Boston.

Much like Billy Sullivan, Angelina was quick to the point and clear in her communication with Ben. She already knew his social skills were essentially absent, but she suspected he had much more to offer that would make up for the deficiency. She decided she would do most of the talking, which suited Ben perfectly fine. The conversation with Angelina was a wonderful relief for Ben. He was worried about being awkward and shy and blowing any chance he had with her, but she eased his mind almost immediately. She playfully teased him if he was too quiet when answering her questions and corrected his gaze if he spoke to her while staring at the floor or wall. Angelina's warm smile made it easy for Ben to forget all about his bashful nature. In no time at all, Ben was picking up the conversation where Angelina left off and speaking with her like the two had been friends since childhood. Ben was animated, even loud at times and the regular patrons and staff at the Firehouse were caught up in the moment. They watched Angelina effortlessly produce such a welcome response from Ben, something many of them had wanted to see but had given up on months prior. Even strangers couldn't help but notice what a lovely young couple the two of them made, not knowing this was their first meaningful conversation together. The mutually tantalizing conversation continued until closing time, which was much later than Ben ever stayed at the Firehouse on Thursday evenings.

Ben was high on the moment on his drive home from the bar, a half-hour drive on the George Washington Memorial Parkway along the Potomac River. Ben loved driving the Parkway home from the bar and work; the Parkway ended at George Washington's Mount Vernon Estate where he took a side road the rest of the way home. Most of Ben's colleagues were confused about why the young man would ever drive to work in the DC traffic as often as he did. Ben could drive fifteen minutes from Mount Vernon and park for $4.95 a day at either the Huntington Metro station to the northeast, and take the Yellow Line, or the Franconia-Springfield station to the northwest, and take the Blue Line, saving time, money, and frustration. His coworkers didn't understand the feeling Ben got driving his Jeep Wrangler, nor did they share his passion for the historic scenery along the way. The slow, solitary commute also allowed him time to think and relieved whatever stress he was feeling. He would often talk to himself in traffic jams, or turn the radio up loud and sing along if he was in the right mood. These were things he would never admit to his coworkers, nor attempt on the Metro. Ben drove most of the time and didn't mind the slow ride one bit.

The shy young man from Arkansas was singing along with the radio and feeling more alive than he ever remembered since coming to the nation's capital. The pretty girl from Boston named Angel who he never believed would reach him beyond fantasy blasted through his defenses in one swift and delightful assault. The reality of their conversation had surpassed any of those in his imagination leading up to tonight. Ben was hooked, he was a goner; he knew it and he was thoroughly enjoying it. Ben left the bar with Angelina's number on his phone and a promise to call her when he got home so she knew he made it OK.

The love-struck Ben Gilsum was also supposed to think about when and where he would like to see Angelina again during his ride home. Ben had already thought of a few ideas long before he was given the task of considering a location for a first date, as this was something he had fantasized they would talk about. There were plenty of romantic places in Old Town and in DC where a couple of young professionals could enjoy each other's company. Ben discussed the options out loud, talking to himself as he often did in his Jeep, "We could go to Le Refuge in Old Town. Ooh, la la! Very fancy, very French. Authentic Parisian cuisine, Mademoiselle?" Ben thought a moment, shrugged, and continued with other options, "But Angel is pretty high class. Maybe 1789 in DC? Very upscale. Beautiful atmosphere for a beautiful girl? I love that building, lots of history. It'd give me something to talk about." Ben continued the conversation all the way home. He was quiet and shy, but he was thoughtful and would prove to be quite romantic when the right person in the right moment came along, and that's exactly what was happening.

Chapter 12

Ben called Angelina when he got home, as she requested, to let her know he got home safe. He called again Friday. And on Saturday night they were on the phone until 2:30 in the morning, chatting like love-sick teenagers. When Sunday rolled around for Ben it included sleeping in late. Ben spent the day catching up on chores and watching whatever sport was in season on TV. Some Sundays he would venture out to go shopping or visit one of many museums in the area. Ben enjoyed reading about history, but given his location and proximity to so many terrific monuments and museums, he would often spend his Sundays visiting and touching actual relics of history. Today, the exhausted but happy Ben Gilsum was content to spend the day relaxing and watching Sports Center. It had been a long and eventful week for Ben and he deserved this day to relax and enjoy feeling terrific about what was happening in his life. His quiet home in the woods was the perfect setting to enjoy his own feelings and emotions without distraction from the rest of the world. Ben thrived on this time, alone in the woods to reset his mood.

Ben had just begun to fall asleep on the couch when his doorbell rang. *Who the hell is that!?* Ben was greeted at the door by two men, both formally dressed and smiling back at him in a way that suggested they knew him and that he would be expecting their visit. They were an odd pair, one approximately Ben's age and the other far older. The younger man was wearing a fashionable and expensive-looking suit with perfectly shined shoes. He looked like a young version of Mr. White, with his dark hair slicked back in a way that suggested he wanted to look good but had no time for styling his hair. The older man was much older, at least in his eighties, also dressed well but a little less formal with wool trousers and a sweater over a collared shirt and no tie. He wore sneakers that scuffed the ground as he walked because he had trouble lifting his feet fully off the ground between steps. Ben stared at them both, unable to hide the puzzled look on his face as he wondered what religious literature they were about to hand him.

"Can I help you?" Ben asked.

"Ben, it's Billy Sullivan from the Brothers of Herrad," the younger man replied. "It's great to meet you, please say hello to my friend and fellow brother, Mr. James."

Ben had completely forgotten that he agreed to allow Billy to send a couple members of the Brothers to discuss his membership. He was frozen for a moment, unable to think of what to say or to find his manners and invite the men into his home. As he had done during their last conversation, Billy saved Ben from his moment of temporary panic, "Ben would it be all right if we came in to discuss your request to join the Brothers of Herrad? Is this a bad time?" Ben quickly regained his composure and invited the men inside.

He offered them a drink, which Billy politely declined. Mr. James was staring at Ben in a way that made Ben feel a little uncomfortable. Ben had a feeling that Mr. James was completely fascinated with him, as if Ben was some unusual animal at a zoo exhibit he was seeing for the first time live and admiring in person. Mr. James asked for water, which Ben brought to him as the three men sat down in the small living room. Ben turned the television off and sat focused on Billy, whose gaze wasn't nearly as awkward. The men sat in silence looking at one another and as usual, someone other than Ben was the first to speak.

"Before we start I wanted you to know that it's unusual for me to attend these meetings personally," Billy said. "We normally send a new officer along with another member to interview potential candidates for initiation and they report back during the next assembly, where a vote by the full membership determines how we proceed."

Ben wasn't sure where this was going, but he didn't get any sense from Billy that there was negativity coming. While Mr. James was clearly admiring Ben, Billy was far more at ease. He presented himself as a figure of authority who was about to praise a subordinate for doing something well though his manner was still a bit robotic. Ben had a sense that this interview would go well regardless of what came next.

Billy continued, "Because you and I got along so well on the phone, I volunteered myself to conduct this interview. It was discussed among the officers and agreed it would be best if you met with someone familiar first. You've come to us on your own and not by a recommendation from another member, which is always the case, and this presents us with an unusual but intriguing first meeting. I'm happy to meet you and Mr. James, who is our most senior member, was also excited to volunteer to come and possibly be your mentor, something he hasn't done in many years. When Mr. James heard about you he insisted he be first to meet you and should your interview go well, he insisted that he would be your mentor."

Oh, that's just great. He's gonna pair me up with this guy? Why is this creepy old man staring at me like that!?

With the formalities taken care of, it was time to begin the interview. Ben was a little nervous and still curious about the Brothers. He expected he would have time to ask a few questions of his own. Mr. James was the first to ask a question and his demeanor had become more professional. Following his intuitive ability, Ben was warming up to Mr. James. He had a friendly smile and an elegant nature about him. Ben imagined Mr. James had either been quite successful in his younger life or raised in a highly sophisticated environment. He was smart and kind, his discourse was polished and filled with wisdom. Ben was beginning to believe Mr. James would be an excellent mentor and it seemed obvious Mr. James liked Ben as well.

"Ben, I've gathered that you're not a married man. Can you tell us a little about your family life? Do you intend to be married one day? Perhaps start a family of your own?" Ben wasn't surprised they got right to the point or that the questions were personal. He expected it. He answered no, he was not married. He wanted to be married someday, but wasn't in a romantic relationship, at least not yet, and he had always hoped to be a father one day.

The next series of questions came from Billy. Would the financial requirements that came with membership, which were minimal, be a burden to him or his family? Would the time spent volunteering, training, and going to meetings put any stress on him or his family? Had he discussed his desire for membership with his family and are they comfortable with his decision? All practical questions and easy answers for Ben, who was independent and though he sent money to his parents in Arkansas frequently, they did not depend on him financially. He was free to take this journey without concern of any hardship for anyone else.

Billy then turned to Mr. James who asked more personal questions, "Ben do you believe in God?" Ben was slow to answer, admitting he wasn't a religious man but that he always believed in a higher power. He often prayed, though he wasn't sure who he was praying to. A warm smile from Mr. James made Ben feel more comfortable with what he believed was a half-assed answer. *Phew!* "Have you ever been convicted of a crime?" *No.* "Have you ever committed a crime or been involved in felonious activity?" *Not exactly.*

Ben answered, "No, I have a perfect record. I've never even gotten a speeding ticket and I've never committed a crime."

Mr. James continued, "Ben are you addicted to any drugs or alcohol?"

"No." Mr. James continued to smile at Ben. He was done asking questions and seemed satisfied with Ben's answers. Over the course of the interview, Ben had gotten the feeling that Mr. James knew something about him. It seemed as if he knew something perhaps Ben didn't even know or understand himself. While he was asking apparently routine questions, the answers didn't really seem to matter. Mr. James was looking at Ben like he was reading his expressions and even his thoughts. Thankfully, he appeared to be completely satisfied. Still, it left Ben a bit uneasy and wondering what was happening.

The last question went back to Billy, "Ben, you're doing great. It's really a pleasure meeting you and learning more about you. We only have one more question for you. Can you please tell us why you're interested in becoming a member of the Brothers of Herrad?"

Ben was expecting this one. He took the time to explain exactly why he had sought out the Brothers, leaving out, of course, how he had gotten their contact information. He was telling the truth while carefully leaving out a slightly tarnished detail. Both of the men seemed thrilled with the answer and thankfully the question of how he found them wasn't asked.

When the conversation came to an end and it was clear there were no further questions, Ben attempted to start asking the questions he had about the Brothers, but Billy quickly stood up and extended his hand, "Ben, that's it, my friend. See, that was painless right?"

Ben tried again to speak, but he was quickly cut off, "Well Mr. James, it's time we leave Mr. Gilsum alone to enjoy what's left of his Sunday."

The old man looked at his **Patek Philippe, Rose Gold Automatic wristwatch, nodded in agreement and** stood up slowly, shaking as he rose. Without another word, the two men made their way to the door.

Ben followed them out and stood just outside the open front door as they started their way to Billy's car, a clean and finely detailed Mercedes S-Class Sedan. After helping Mr. James into the passenger seat, Billy turned to Ben, "Ben, you did very well. Mr. James and I will discuss our interview and present the results during our assembly in a couple weeks with the rest of the membership. I intend to recommend you for initiation and I fully expect Mr. James will second. A ceremonial yet critical vote will take place, which I expect will be a unanimous yes, and you'll be informed of what comes next by Mr. James who will prove to be an extraordinary mentor. Relax Ben, you're now very likely to become part of something special. No regrets, my friend!" And with that, he got into his exceptionally fine-looking, expensive car and drove away. *Why do I feel like I'm being asked to sell puppies with Tommy?*

Chapter 13

Ben didn't have to think very hard about plans for his first date with Angelina. He'd wanted to share the parts of Alexandria he loved with someone since he first arrived, and now he had exceptional company from out of town. Angelina seemed excited about touring King Street, but then Angelina Rindge approached everything with a sense of contagious enthusiasm. It was one of the things Ben adored about her, and something he sorely needed to complement his lack of eagerness for adventure.

Angelina lived in the Rosemont section of Alexandria, about a ten-minute drive northwest of Old Town. She lived alone in a modern-style, brand-new town house, complete with three bedrooms and a personal garage underneath the unit. Her home was in a beautiful building and Ben was impressed as he walked up to ring the doorbell. *It must be good to work for a senator!* When Angelina came to the door, Ben's admiration of the fancy architecture was immediately halted and his attention was drawn exclusively toward the vision of Angelina in an elegant, short, form-fitting black dress. Her long, brown hair was down and styled especially for the evening. The normally silent Ben did not fail to tell his date how amazing she looked as he opened the door to his Jeep for her to climb aboard,

Brian D. Campbell

which earned him a kiss on the cheek as a reward for the compliment. "Thanks, babe. You don't look so bad either!" *Babe?*

King Street is the main street in Alexandria's Old Town complete with many historic buildings and plenty of historic sites. Attractions include the George Washington Masonic National Memorial, which Ben assumed would interest Angelina given her family history with Freemasons, as well as King Street Gardens Park, which showcased vine-covered structures built to honor George Washington. Several beautiful and historic museums in this area include George Washington's town house, torn down but rebuilt in 1960, which was used to accommodate visitors to Mount Vernon.

It was early spring and the weather was clear, dry, and perfect for the young couple. Ben would prove to be an excellent tour guide on the path he had walked many times alone, often wishing to have someone as lovely as Angelina to accompany him. The two would walk King Street, take in the sites and end with dinner and drinks in one of the many local taverns or restaurants.

One site Ben would sometimes stop at was a statue of a Confederate soldier created by Caspar Buberl, based on a figure in a painting by John Elder titled "Appomattox," erected in 1889. The statue is a lone soldier viewing the aftermath of the battle of Appomattox Court House where Robert E. Lee surrendered to Ulysses S. Grant. The statue's base includes names of Alexandrians who died for the Confederacy. The monument itself is actually located in the center of an intersection, so a brief stop and description were all Ben could offer. He was unsure what a girl from Boston might think about a Confederate statue, but was determined to stop and show her because it was just a short walk off the path and he wanted to show her all of his adopted home. The statue had meaning for Ben because to him it symbolized the end of a terrible chapter in U.S. history. He wondered how Angelina would respond.

Ben assumed that since Angelina was just out of college and from New England, she might be offended by the site of a Confederate statue, especially given recent events and press coverage on the topic. He was hoping for a revealing reaction from his companion. As a person who enjoyed observing the behavior of people around him, Ben couldn't resist the experiment even on a first date. Though Ben was quite political and had his own strong and well-developed opinions, he never allowed current events or flash topics, which he considered fringe sentiment, to get him too excited. The young history buff had a lesson prepared that he hoped would impress his lovely new friend. Angelina came from an influential family in the Boston area that was heavily involved in politics and connected with politicians. Her father was friends with people at all levels of government and those friends were never shy about building relationships with the Rindge family or seeking donations. As Ben suspected, Angelina was quite liberal.

The beautiful young woman from Boston wore a smile the entire evening, but stopped at the monument with a more subdued and curious expression, "Well this is a bit of a downer, Ben. I'm honestly surprised this thing hasn't been torn down yet. Are you sure you want to spend time looking at this?"

Ben laughed. He could tell Angelina was half kidding and not bothered by the existence of the monument. It was the response he was expecting, and he had given a great deal of thought about how he would answer when asked this question. Ben paused as they crossed the intersection and turned looking back at the statue, "Believe me, I have no love for Confederate soldiers. I mean, I have a personal stake in the demise of the Confederate States of America. As far as tearing this statue down, I like to think of history as a story that's never done being told. There's no real beginning either. The story is always incomplete. The story of this statue isn't over yet. Maybe it includes being torn down, maybe it doesn't. The locals say tearing it down would be erasing history, but I think if it's torn down that's just a part of the story that hasn't been told yet. You can never erase history Angel, all you can ever hope to do is learn from it."

Angelina looked puzzled, "I guess I assumed you were more of a liberal."

Ben was prepared for that too. "I guess I don't really know where I stand politically," Ben lied. "To me it's wrong to look at history from a political perspective because politics change with the times. Today's conservatives are yesterday's liberals. Trying to apply a political perspective to history is never a good idea, it tends to sway the facts and I don't think we should ever do that. Think of the founding fathers for example. Conservatives today claim them as their own and maybe based on today's politics that's appropriate, but in the times of our founding fathers, they would have been considered the most liberal people on Earth. The notion that a peasant was just as important as a king? The concept that everyone had equal human rights? 'We hold these truths to be self-evident, that all men are created equal, that they are endowed by their Creator with certain unalienable Rights, that among these are Life, Liberty and the pursuit of Happiness' This was pretty progressive stuff in the seventeen hundreds!" Ben sensed he was going too far, so he decided to quit while he was ahead, "I mean, I know those guys owned slaves, treated women like property, and did all sorts of things that would be considered criminal by today's standards, but they gave humankind a spark that endured and changed the world forever. What you're seeing today is just a continuation of what they started two-hundred and fifty years ago and the story isn't done being told."

Angelina's smile returned, which brought Ben quickly out of his deep reflection at the old bronze monument, and he gave a smile of his own. "Ben Gilsum, you sir are a romantic. And you're full of surprises my friend. I'm not gonna lie Ben, it's actually kinda sexy." And with that, the young couple shared their first kiss.

Success! Angelina had the exact response Ben was hoping she would. Now it was time to wrap up the tour with dinner and see where the night might lead. Their path on King Street and over to the Appomattox Statue on Prince had led them within a half block of the Columbia Firehouse, but the two decided tonight they wanted to spend the evening elsewhere. They backtracked about five blocks to Vermilion, an elegant American restaurant with a local chef and farm-to-table fare.

The young couple dined upstairs, away from the bar for a more intimate atmosphere. As they dined and drank, the two picked up where they left off during their last encounter. Ben was free from his previously impenetrable shell and Angelina was rewarded with the person she knew existed behind all the quiet mystery that was once Ben Gilsum. It seemed Ben's life was changing on all facets and he was powerless to slow it down. The once overly cautious Ben Gilsum, who missed many an opportunity by overthinking and not reacting naturally, was moving at hyper speed on what appeared to be a course filled with beauty and wonder. He wasn't sure yet if he should worry, but he wasn't about to hit the brakes. Ben was happy, and on this night he was rewarded for letting go of his reservations.

At the end of the best first date Ben believed he'd ever experienced, he pulled over to the side of the street in front of Angelina's town house and quickly got out of his Jeep, anxiously walking around to open the door for his date, "Hold on, Angel, I got it." The young man's heart was racing as he anticipated another kiss to end the perfect evening.

"You're adorable, Ben," Angelina said with a provocative smile after she stepped out onto the sidewalk, inviting her date to claim the kiss he was hoping for. "Ben, Babe...Would you like to come inside with me?" Angelina asked softly.

Chapter 14

U ntil all the recent excitement in Ben's life, he was living in Virginia by a painfully dull and routine schedule. Wednesday night meant time to call home and check in with his parents, though, sadly, there was never anything new to report. The calls had become boring, normally lasting about a half an hour, with long pauses in between the repeated updates on what was happening in both DC and Decatur. The excitement of being near the nation's capital had dulled for both Ben and his parents. There were occasional calls with heated debates about whether his parents could use a little money. Ben would offer his very poor, but stubborn father money, but Mr. Gilsum would insist his son save it for himself for when he needed it. Other calls would go on hold as Mrs. Gilsum couldn't hold back the tears for missing her beloved son. Those calls were the hardest for Ben. He sorely missed his mother, perhaps as much as she missed him.

This call was different. Ben had been looking forward to his scheduled call home for the first time in a while. He had something exciting he couldn't wait to share with his mother. He knew how happy it would make her to hear he wouldn't be spending so much time alone anymore. Ben had a girlfriend. Ben was falling in love, hard and fast. Mrs. Gilsum would be overjoyed with the news.

Being away from Decatur didn't bother Ben at all, but being away from his mother was hard. Giving his mother this news would make them both happier about the move to Virginia. Ben had several girlfriends growing up, but none of them impressed Mrs. Gilsum. No one was ever good enough for her beloved Benjamin. Ben knew she felt that way and rarely introduced any of his girlfriends to his mother to avoid the cold brush-off that was sure to greet them. It was hard enough for Ben to bring friends home due to the state of poverty his family lived in.

Angelina Rindge was different. Her smile was contagious, her energy was positive and brilliant. She was beautiful, but what she did for Ben was something that would bring a tear to his mother's eye. She made him human and Mrs. Gilsum would undoubtedly fall in love with her for that.

Mrs. Gilsum answered the phone after the typical two rings, "Hi, baby, your father's here and we have you on the speaker."

Ben didn't understand why, but his mother never answered the phone on the first ring. Even if she was waiting by the phone, which on Wednesday evenings she always was, she never answered the phone until after at least two rings. "Hi Mom, hi Dad. How are things back home?" Ben waited through the normal questions and answers about how things were going and for a pause in conversation to share his exciting news.

"Mom, I met a girl," Ben started after the small talk had ended.

"Oh, baby that's wonderful. Is this someone you met at work?" Mrs. Gilsum asked.

"No, Mom, I met her volunteering at the youth center." Ben lied because "at a bar" would surely not please Mrs. Gilsum in the least.

Mrs. Gilsum was perked up and firing questions faster than Ben could answer. "That's great, Ben, what's her name? How long have you been seeing her? Is it serious?"

"Her name is Angel, Mom, and she's incredible. You would love her, Mom, you really would," Ben stopped with just that answer to the rapid-fire questions from his excited yet cautious mother who clearly wanted to know if he'd been keeping her a secret and if so for how long.

"Ben, you're going to make me cry, baby, I'm so happy for you. How long have you and Angel been seeing each other?" she persisted.

"Mom, just a few days really. I mean I met her a while ago, but we've only had one date. We've really just started getting to know each other. She's amazing, Mom, I wish you could meet her." Ben immediately regretted the last part of his comments because the reminder of the distance between them would make his mother sad, especially now. He also had a sudden fear of bringing Angelina to Arkansas to see where he came from. *No way in hell that's ever going to happen.*

Mr. Gilsum broke his typical silence, "Ben, son, you be careful up there. You've only just met this girl, and it seems to me you're moving pretty fast already. Easy there, son, don't you go selling puppies." *Wait until he finds out she's from Massachusetts, a Yankee no less!*

"I know Dad...," Ben started but was quickly cut off by his mother who would have none of this from her husband, the man who never trusted anyone.

"Now, Ben, you pay no attention to your father. Trust your heart baby, God and *your mother* gave you a good one. If Angel makes you feel this way, then she really is an Angel. She sounds wonderful Ben, and I wish we could meet her, too. Maybe someday soon we will, give it time and enjoy yourselves. This is beautiful, baby, I'm so happy to hear this news. Don't you overthink this and pay no mind to your father. Don't spend so much time analyzing humans that you forget to be one. Trust your heart for once and give your mind a rest, baby."

Mr. Gilsum as always had nothing further to add and his wife appeared to have no further questions about Angel. With the break in conversation, Ben decided to wrap up the call and wish his parents a good night.

Chapter 15

For a while Ben had been wanting to ask his boss Ted what he knew of the Brothers of Herrad, especially since he could not find anything on his own, even using the sophisticated communication collecting and analyzing software at the company. He had been putting it off because of his recent indiscretion using company and U.S. Government resources for that purpose. Ben was afraid Ted may have noticed the unauthorized search but hadn't had the opportunity to ask him about it yet. *I'd love to pick Ted's brain about these guys, but what if he's waiting for the right time to ask me about my unauthorized searches? What if when I ask him about the Brothers of Herrad, he remembers he needs to ask me about them?* After enough time Ben determined it was safe to ask. *If Ted hasn't come to me by now about my searches, then I think I'm safe.*

Ben approached Ted in his office and sat down in the black executive-style chair Ted left in front of his desk for his frequent visitors to sit and talk about work, baseball, or anything else that was on their mind. Most people in the office, Ben included, would just steal a rigid back-breaking conference room chair from somewhere in the building to use as an extra in their office, but Ted convinced the office manager he needed something more comfortable and welcoming. That thoughtful behavior was typical for Ted. He was very well-respected and liked throughout the company and there was often someone seated in the chair that had become known as "the therapy chair." Anyone who had problems of any kind would sit and talk them out with the beloved department head.

Ben started with the usual sports talk and then changed the topic during the first natural pause in conversation, "So I've been thinking about joining a group that's a lot like the Freemasons, but no one's ever heard of them. They're called the Brothers of Herrad. They do a lot of volunteer work and donate to a bunch of local causes and things like that. I met a couple of them over at the Boys and Girls Club where I coach on Saturdays. You ever heard of them?"

Ted stared at Ben silently for what seemed like forever, almost to a point of nervousness for Ben. Ted finally spoke, "I have heard of them, but only in relation to some projects we've done here. Nothing exciting, seem like a bunch of adult boy scouts to me. Nothing we've looked into ever amounted to anything more than that."

For the first time since he met Ted, Ben got the impression he wasn't being honest. It was as plain as the look on his face to Ben. Ted was lying and he wasn't a very good liar. Ben tried to hide his own nervousness about the obvious lie but felt like he was failing miserably. He stared at the floor, the ceiling, looking anywhere he could to avoid Ted's eyes.

Ted continued, offering his opinion of secret societies, particularly those in the DC area. He took a deep breath, leaned forward, put his hands together as if in prayer with his elbows on his desk and placed his pointer fingers over his lips and his thumbs under his chin and stared at Ben who was positively fidgeting while trying to avoid eye contact with his boss. After a few seconds he exhaled, lowered his hands and spoke, "Ben I think it's great that you spend so much time volunteering and are looking for an outlet to do more of that. Let me give you some friendly advice about some of these organizations. Here in DC, anyone connected to anyone or anything with any semblance of status or power, influence, or usefulness of any sort needs to be very careful who they associate with. As you gain any of these things, whether it be through your career or other endeavors, you become more valuable and that makes you more desirable to others with both good and bad intentions. You'll eventually notice that it seems everyone here in town is connected in some way to power or influence or usefulness. I can't stress enough that you should be careful who you associate with. You have so much to offer, Ben. That fact makes you a target for those with bad intentions. And you may not know of those intentions until it's too late. Try to learn as much as you can about anyone you become associated with before you become too connected to them. Sometimes even a causal connection with the right or wrong person can be used as currency in this town."

Ben spent the rest of the day in a haze. Why was Ted lying about the Brothers? What did he know about them? Why did Ted feel the need to warn him about them while lying that he knew so little about them? Should he tell Billy and Mr. James that he changed his mind about wanting to be a member? Had he gotten himself into trouble? For the first time since meeting Billy and Angelina, Ben had returned to a state he was far more familiar with. He was overanalyzing every thought and decision to the point where he had no idea what to do next.

Chapter 16

S pending time with Angelina had become the top priority for Ben; their relationship had grown quite strong. The young couple spent their weekends making Washington, DC, and its parks and monuments their playground. Angelina did a great job keeping things light and fun. When Ben got too long-winded explaining the history of a monument or statue, the always playful Angelina would mock him and tease him. "Oh, really, babe? That's very interesting. Can you repeat ALL of that because NO ONE CARES!" This would be followed with a playful push, or a jab and a kiss. Most of the time Ben would get the hint, but sometimes he couldn't help himself. Angelina understood that and admired his passion. She would encourage it on occasion, "Actually, you're kinda hot when you're being smart and all serious, babe, tell me more. If I had you for a professor, I'd have aced Early U.S. History at Dartmouth for sure! "

One Saturday, as they walked the sidewalks around the National Mall, Ben pointed and said to Angelina, "Look at that couple on those ridiculous scooters!" Ben was pointing out a couple about their same age riding a pair of dockless, electric miniscooters that can be rented in DC by using an app on a cellphone for $1 and then $.15 a mile. "Those stupid things are everywhere now, there's like three different companies renting them out. They're literally parked all over the city. I think it's the same in a few cities."

Angelina smiled, "I think they're cute!"

Much to Ben's horror, his beautiful girlfriend showed up at his apartment the next Saturday with a pair of matching electric scooters and helmets she bought rather than rented. "Are you ready, babe? The city awaits!"

After a couple weeks Ben had forgotten his worries about the Brothers of Herrad and Ted's warning. His attention had been diverted to a much more satisfying place and for the first time since coming to DC, Ben was truly happy. He had given Ted's warning a great deal of thought and determined he had nothing to lose or gain personally in regard to his association with the Brothers of Herrad. Ben had done his homework as well as anyone could be expected to, even more so using highly sophisticated software that most people have no access to. Ben determined he would continue on his current path and learn what he could in the moment.

Staying acutely aware of everything he saw and heard would be his way of heeding Ted's warning. Besides, Ben was intrigued by the mystery of the organization and wanted to know more. He kept telling himself he was free to leave the group at any point if he noticed anything he wouldn't want to be a part of so, there was really no risk. Ben had returned with little effort to the state he was in before speaking with Ted about the Brothers. He would enjoy some adventure and try not to overthink things. This was the same advice his mother had given him when she learned about Angelina, and so far, following it had improved Ben's life immeasurably.

Chapter 17

H ome alone on another lazy Sunday morning watching Sports Center, half-awake, Ben heard a faint tapping at his front door. The first time he heard it he gave it little thought and didn't move from his spot on the couch. A few moments later there was another slightly louder tapping. *What the hell!?* Ben got up and peaked out a window to get a look at what was out there. He saw the frail frame of Mr. James wearing his wool trousers, sweater, and sneakers, looking right at him with a friendly smile on his aged face. This time he was alone or at least Ben didn't see anyone else with him. *The old man drove himself!?* Mr. James gave a wave and continued his smile to make sure Ben knew he was waiting to come in.

Ben opened the door to greet his visitor, looking around outside to see if there was anyone else with him. *Holy shit! The old man did drive himself!*

"Good morning, Ben, I hope I'm not disturbing you," Mr. James said trying to steal Ben's gaze back from the walkway and driveway.

"I have exciting news for you Ben, and I'm not one to share exciting news on the telephone, I'm old-fashioned my young friend. I've discovered that the simple joys in life, like seeing a friend's reaction in person when you share good news with them, makes the trip worth taking."

Aside from the awkwardness Ben felt during their first encounter, Ben had quickly come to admire the old man. "Mr. James, you're always welcome. It's nice to see you again. Please come in and make yourself comfortable. Can I get you anything?"

Mr. James took a glass of water and helped himself to a seat at Ben's table-for-two that was the only physical separation between the kitchen and living room of Ben's small apartment at the old farmhouse property. Ben sat down at the table with his new friend and couldn't help but chuckle to himself at the closeness of the two men at the small table. Ben was used to dining here alone. He and Angelina hadn't yet had the pleasure of sharing a meal together in Mount Vernon. The cozy space suited Mr. James quite well as it made it easier for the older man to hear his friend. Plus, getting up and down from a seat on the couch was not a pleasant experience for a man Ben assumed was well into his 80s.

Mr. James sat smiling at Ben, gathering his strength and drinking his water. Then he finally spoke, "Ben, as I said before I have good news for you. My Brothers agreed at our Assembly last month to allow you to petition for membership. That means you and I have work to do young man, but it's a worthy chore and I'm excited to be the one to help you through it." Another pause as Mr. James stopped speaking to catch his breath and take a sip from his water.

"If you're up for it, you and I have just short of two months to prepare you for initiation. What that means is, you will stand with me before the other officers prior to Assembly and recite the history that forms the core of our Brotherhood. It's what we're all about and how we came to be. These are the principles of the organization, why we do what we do, and why we've devoted our lives to charity and the advancement of humankind."

Ben stayed focused on Mr. James and had yet to speak. He expected this visit. After a wide range of thoughts, from the initial excitement to join the group to heeding Ted's warning and calling the whole thing off, he was determined to continue on the adventure until he found reason not to. He listened intently to Mr. James and nodded occasionally to confirm he was following along.

Mr. James continued after another pause, "So, Ben, if you accept this opportunity, I'd like to propose we meet weekly, Sunday if that works for you, and go over the history I mentioned. We're a private organization, I will need your promise to keep everything we discuss to yourself. You must agree to tell no one anything we talk about in our meetings. This is critical if we are to continue. There are other rules to being a member, but that's the most important for the time being. We'll discuss the others as we go. Once we've completed the training, and you're ready to petition for initiation, you'll stand before the officers like I said. There are no more votes but you must prove yourself worthy of initiation. The officers will voice any doubts or ask questions they feel necessary and your answers will hopefully satisfy them. Once the petition is over, you will leave and we then decide openly with a verbal confirmation at Assembly if there's going to be an initiation. If yes, you come back in seven days and there's a ceremony where you become a member. Sounds easy enough, right?"

Ben took a minute to summarize what he heard and consider the fact that he'd have a date with Mr. James for the next seven or eight Sundays. He then realized this was his first actual opportunity to ask questions about the Brothers. "So, what happens if I become a member? How often do you meet? Are there dues to pay or a certain number of volunteer hours to commit to? What will be expected of me?"

Mr. James just smiled at Ben as he asked his many questions. When it seemed Ben was done, he answered, "The Brothers meet regularly once a month for what we call Assembly. That happens on the first Wednesday of every month. Attendance will be required of you for a few months and then there are no restrictions. We do have less formal meetings that are typically small groups of Brothers working on some specific project who want to coordinate their efforts. At Assembly, we discuss larger issues at hand and focus on our development as an organization. You will be expected to pay a membership fee of two-hundred and fifty dollars for initiation and after that there are no dues. This is more a formality than a practicality, we want to be sure your intentions are sincere. There are no requirements once you're an accepted member. Members put in as much effort as they choose and take away as much benefit as they need. Our hope as an organization is always that both effort and benefit will be plentiful and I have a feeling in your case they will. What was your last question, Ben? No don't answer that, I've got it."

Mr. James fixed his gaze into Ben's eyes, his typically smiling face looking more serious, "What is expected of you? Well, my friend. That's completely up to you. If you tell me you're ready, you're going to learn the true answer and how it can change your life in ways you've never imagined. You have limitless potential, you can do anything. Do you remember what Billy said to you last time we were here? 'Relax Ben, you're now likely to become part of something special.' I don't think I could say it much better than that."

The eager student told his mentor he was ready to accept the invitation. Ben promised that everything they discussed would be confidential, and he wrote a check to the Brothers of Herrad for two-hundred and fifty dollars. The two agreed to meet again in one week at Ben's apartment to begin the training. Ben then walked his aged friend to his car, a beautiful Bentley Continental GT. *Who the hell are these guys!?* Ben stood in the driveway and watched Mr. James pull away, waving just until he was out of sight. *I can't believe that old man can drive.*

Chapter 18

Thursday nights at the Firehouse were no longer spent in quiet reflection and observation of the surrounding life while he dined alone. Ben's lovely dinner companion had changed all of his routines and his weekly ritual for food and beer had not been spared. He still almost always ordered the same dinner, grilled chicken-Caesar salad with a side of kale and white bean soup. He still sometimes strayed and ordered the Firehouse burger and beer-battered onion rings with chipotle mayo when he was extra hungry. And on very rare occasions, the fit and athletic young man would go for the smoked pork ribs and cornbread because it reminded him of home. With the exception of dinner choices, Ben's experiences at the Firehouse had changed completely. He realized that with Angelina sitting across from him, people were doing more than just giving him a friendly smile and hello as the typical failed attempt to break down his barrier. He was becoming a part of the life and stories that were happening there. People were opening up to him and he was finding no trouble responding to them as he had in the past. Ben was making friends, which is something he hadn't done since he left Decatur.

Angelina had news for Ben and she was bouncing off her seat with excitement to tell him about it. Angelina was close to her father and kept in constant communication with him. She had told him about this new guy she was spending time with and that things were getting serious. Angelina's father, Mr. Rindge, was a wealthy and powerful man who had worked very hard to become so. He had friends in high places throughout Boston and in DC. His influence and connections had helped Angelina land her job working for a senator from their home state of Massachusetts.

During her last phone call home, Mr. Rindge expressed concern to his only daughter about this new friend. "Angel, you know how I feel about Washington. And you're in a position there due to your association with a senator to attract all kinds of bad people with all kinds of bad intentions. I'm not comfortable with you getting too close with ANYONE down there."

As Angelina protested, her father stopped her, "Look, sweetie, indulge your father, will you? You know I could just ask some of my friends to keep an eye on you in that cesspool, but if you care for him as much as you say you do, that will not be enough for me. I need to meet him, immediately."

Angelina tried again to interrupt her father with a counterargument, but he persisted, "Hear me out, Angel. I will not be a tyrant to your boyfriend. I just want to meet him, and make sure you're OK."

Mr. Rindge changed his tone to playful, "Maybe scare him just a little. Put the fear of God into him. Make him disappear discreetly if he's not who he says he is? You know, typical loving father stuff? Why not invite him home for a weekend?"

Mr. Rindge would get his way. Mr. Rindge always got his way, "Oh, Daddy, of course you can meet him. And be nice! You're going to love him."

Ben's demeanor changed promptly from happy and excited about being with Angelina to panic. *She wants me to go to Boston to meet her parents!?* "You really wanna bring your boyfriend from the south, the boonies of Arkansas, home with you to Boston to meet your senator-father?"

Angelina's enthusiasm was unaltered by Ben's feeble attempt. "My father is not a senator and he's going to love you! My family isn't like that. And by the way, we love the south. You say things like 'Oh, bless your heart!' and we eat it up. It'll be awesome."

Ben couldn't help but correct his beautiful girlfriend, "What your family doesn't realize is when a person from the south says 'Oh, bless your heart!' they're really thinking 'Oh, go fuck yourself!' They just don't wanna say it out loud. Don't let Southern charm and the cute little sayings they use fool you."

Angelina ignored her boyfriend and proceeded to inform him he needed to clear a weekend and soon so they could book a trip to Boston. All expenses were to be covered by her father and it was going to be awesome. It didn't take long for Ben to realize it was pointless to resist. Angelina was accustomed to getting what she wanted and Ben was powerless to stop her. He had also learned that pleasing Angelina was well worth the effort. *Let the adventure continue!*

Chapter 19

Mr. James arrived exactly the time he said he would on Sunday morning, alone again, wearing his signature wool trousers and sneakers. He was ready to start Ben's training for membership into the Brothers of Herrad. This time Ben was expecting his mentor and greeted him at the door before he knocked. The old man seemed excited, full of energy, and eager to get started. He asked for his usual glass of water and nothing else. Ben joined him at the small dining room table eager to finally hear more about the Brothers.

Mr. James started by telling Ben why he had joined the group so many years ago. "Ben, when I was a young man like you, I started my professional life as a bank teller in Boston. This was a noble position in those days and I did very well. I had ambitions for more and eventually I worked my way up with the bank I started at and made a very good life for myself and my family. I've lived a very comfortable life, but I've always been aware of the suffering of those less fortunate. While those I associated with seemed to have an effortless ability to shrug at the misfortune of others, convinced their condition was a symptom of their own doing, whether it be laziness or addiction of some sort, I could never fully remove myself from it. It would keep me up nights. It was almost as if I could feel their pain, their emotions, and their shame. It was sometimes overwhelming and it would last for days at a time. As I grew older, I taught myself how to control the feelings I was having. When you can feel the suffering of others, it's easy to become motivated to use whatever influence you have to ease it. It was this that motivated me to seek out an organization that could give me the opportunity to help my fellow man, a group of men dedicated specifically to two ambitions. First, to offer their time and energy to help those in their communities in need. And the second ambition, well Mr. Gilsum, we'll be talking about that over the next few weeks. It's the basic philosophy of myself, and my Brothers, that no matter how hard one person tries they cannot change the world alone. The best any of us can do is change ourselves and spread what we've learned to those around us. Then we hope our efforts, our love, and kindness toward our fellow man is recognized and repeated. That's why I'm here, Ben. I feel that I know you so very well. It seems to me, young man, that you and I have so much more in common than you realize."

Ben found himself questioning Mr. James' assumption he was experiencing the same feelings that the older man was describing in his youth. While Ben knew he was acutely aware of a person's emotions and had a special talent for reading a person's intentions and sincerity, he hadn't ever been overwhelmed by the sorrow of others the way Mr. James described. Or had he? Perhaps.

He wanted to do more to help his fellow man and that was definitely motivating him. But the rest? Ben spoke up about this fact and Mr. James said something that caught him by surprise. In fact, it stunned him. "Ben you're an introvert. An extreme case. You avoid taking part in the world around you and just observe from a distance, never allowing yourself to get close to those you don't feel comfortable with. Then you come out here to the woods, far away from others. Have you ever wondered why you behave that way? I think I can explain, Ben. You're protecting yourself. You've learned a long time ago, perhaps so long ago that you don't remember, that the best way to protect yourself from the pain and suffering, even the anger and fear around you, is to disengage. This will need to change young man, and I will help you learn how to better separate yourself from emotions that aren't yours while still being an active and constructive part of your community. You also need to stop shielding yourself from experiencing the joy and love around you son." *How the hell does he know so much about me?*

"Ben, when I learned more about you, I knew you and I had to work together. I haven't been a mentor since before you were born, but I knew I had to mentor you. I'm so happy to be here, Ben. Are you ready to get started?"

The conversation was feeling uncomfortable and Ben jumped at the opportunity to change the subject. *The old man is creeping me out now!* "Yes, Mr. James, I'm eager to learn something about the Brothers of Herrad. I have to admit, you're the most top-secret secret society I've ever heard of. There's nothing about you on the web."

Mr. James smiled, "We're not secret, Ben, and anyone can come and visit our lodge when they want to learn more about us. There's always someone there who would answer questions for them, though we've had very few visitors."

Ben tried to hide the puzzled look on his face when he heard that, remembering his visit to the lodge. No signs, and certainly no warm greeting for a visitor. He continued to listen and try to hide his doubts.

"What we are, Ben," Mr. James continued with a renewed smile, "is a private organization. We operate out in the open all the time, but we keep our inside business private. We're no secret society at all. We're always open to new members, should they meet our criteria."

With that out of the way Mr. James took on a serious tone and began talking about the core beliefs of the Brothers of Herrad. "Let me start with the name of our organization. Why the Brothers of Herrad? Who is Herrad? A special person who lived nearly a thousand years ago. A nun actually. Herrad of Landsberg."

Ben decided not to try again to hide the familiarity of what his mentor was speaking about and interrupted, "Yes, I looked her up before you and Billy came to see me the first time. She's known as the world's first feminist, she was really into science and wrote a book that summarized all the world's collective knowledge of her time. I think it was called the 'Hortus Deliciarum'?"

Mr. James was impressed, though not surprised, "Yes, Ben, you've done your homework, haven't you? That's exactly who she is and part of the reason she's so important to us and to the world. But there was more than just scientific or even religious knowledge that came from the very blessed Herrad of Landsberg. Herrad had collected writings and teachings from all over the world. While Hortus Deliciarum was a wonderful masterpiece, the finished work was slightly incomplete based on her initial hopes. It was determined that some portions of the collection were far too scandalous and not at all in line with the church teachings of the day. So for her protection, she wisely kept some of her findings private. The private pieces of Herrad's collection that later came into the possession of our founding member form the basic purpose of our organization. You and I are going to discuss those findings so you can determine if you'd like to become a member of our group. If you want to join us after what you learn in our sessions, your task at your request for initiation will be to convince our members you understand the importance of those findings and are prepared to dedicate yourself to them and ultimately to your fellow man. If you chose that you don't want to join us, all I ask of you is to keep what you learn to yourself. Remember, we are a private organization and I need your absolute word that what we talk about stays between us."

Ben gave Mr. James his word, as he had done before, that anything they discussed would be kept private. Who would he tell? Who would believe any of it anyway? Ben had read sacred oaths from Freemason initiations that should the initiate discuss private business they agreed they would face having their throat cut, their tongue torn out by its roots, and their body buried in the sands of the sea at low tide. This promise seemed far more reasonable, "I promise, not a word to anyone."

"Excellent, Ben. Now, we'll discuss some things you're likely familiar with and go into further detail about what they actually mean. Please understand that often it's difficult to know for sure if these stories are meant to be taken literally or metaphorically as so much time has passed and translations have been handed down many times. I fully expect you to form your own opinion, I actually encourage it. We're not at Sunday school, Ben. God gave you a beautiful mind and I believe he enjoys watching you use it as much as I do."

Ben knew religion would come into play, as it's a common theme with every secret society he had ever read about. What he didn't know was how strange this was about to become. The freedom to use his mind to form his own opinion was a relief, and he was eager to hear more.

"In ancient times, before Christ walked the Earth, there was God, angels, and man. There was contact between the three, not just spiritual but actual contact between them here on Earth. Man sinned then, much like man sins now, but God would often punish man on Earth. Angels were servants of God and ultimately man. God loved and favored man and this made some angels a bit jealous. One in particular I know you've heard of and who has many names was Satan. Satan grew angry and determined to prove to God that angels deserved his love over man because man had many flaws and continued to fail and falter even when punished by God. It was this anger Satan felt that ultimately led to his banishment from both Earth and Heaven. Satan and the other angels who felt the same anger were transformed into unsightly demons and banished to hell forever, though they would often venture to Earth and cause trouble for man. They still do to this day, though physical contact on Earth is strictly prohibited. Theirs is more a tormenting of mankind with temptation and negative influence." Mr. James stopped and looked at Ben who he could tell was losing focus.

"Well, my young friend, I think the creation of the boundaries between angels, demons, and man is a terrific place to stop. Ben, remember these things we've discussed. Write them down if you have to, repeat them to yourself later. All of this will be up for discussion at your petition for initiation and how well you show you can follow will go a long way."

Write them down? Jotting down notes of private information is strictly forbidden by Freemasons. That's explicitly agreed to by oath. Why are these guys so different? Ben nodded to show his understanding. They didn't get very far and he would easily remember what they talked about so far. *God, the devil, angels, demons. Yeah, got it.* Ben walked his old friend to his car, shook his hand, and waved as he drove off. *What the hell am I getting myself into!?*

Chapter 20

Ben left work early on Thursday. His afternoon did not include making his usual stop at the Columbia Firehouse for dinner. He had to go home, pack, and be ready by three o'clock because Angelina was coming to pick him up and drive them to the airport so they could catch a plane to Boston. Ben would spend Thursday and Friday night at his girlfriend's parents' house, a fact he'd been trying hard to ignore all week. He dreaded forced small talk and probing questions and trying his hardest to not be the shy and awkward person he and everyone who met him instantly knew he was. He kept reminding himself that this was just a necessary part of this beautiful adventure he was on, and at the end of it he would be with Angelina and she would be happy. And Ben really enjoyed being with Angelina, particularly when she was happy. Besides, how bad could it be?

The young couple did not rent a car and there was no family member waiting for them as they left the gate at Logan Airport in Boston. Just a middle-aged woman holding a white sign she had made herself with bright, multicolored letters reading, "Miss Angelina Rindge and Handsome *Gest.*" The sign with the word guest misspelled and the woman with her huge, warm smile were hard to miss; Angelina squealed as they got closer,

"Marta!!!" She ran up to the woman and gave her a hug as a wave of smiles passed by them on both sides of the airport hallway. This was the typical response in most crowded rooms where Angelina was present.

Angelina loved being in a crowd and crowds loved being around Angelina. Ben was the exact opposite and loathed being in a crowd. He became overwhelmed to a point of being dizzy and nauseous when surrounded by a large group of people in a small area. Being in a crowd sometimes felt to Ben like being in the middle of a thousand conversations and he was trying to keep up with all of them at once even though he wasn't part of any of them. This feeling made Ben a wallflower among large groups or parties; it kept him well clear of dance floors. Ben hated to dance. He was much more suited for one-on-one engagements, as he was excellent at listening and conversing with someone he had become comfortable with. Most of Ben's close friends believed he was their most trusted and warmest friend. Ben was a person with few friends, but one who built strong relationships with those select few.

"Hello, my dearest Angel," Marta replied with an Eastern European accent while wrapped in Angelina's hug.

Angelina turned to Ben, "This is Marta. Marta was my nanny, my tutor, my best friend and is all around the most awesome person in the world."

Ben smiled and greeted the short, rotund woman with short brown hair and round face, trying to figure out exactly who she was and what her role was if she was no longer a nanny or a tutor. *Does Angel have a personal assistant!?*

"Hello Marta, I'm Ben," Ben said as he pondered about Marta's current job.

"Well, duh, Ben, you're the tallest, darkest, and most handsome man at the airport. For sure you're Ben. Who else would you be!?" Marta replied.

Ben liked Marta immediately. Though her accent was a little tough to navigate at first, he had little trouble understanding her. She was loud, constantly joking, and she smelled like cinnamon buns. The Rindge family domestic helper from Poland was as joyful and happy as Angelina and as a result, she was impossible to dislike.

"Marta, my darling, you spelled 'guest' wrong on your fabulous sign," Angelina pointed out.

"What do you mean, my lovely?" Marta questioned, holding up her sign and looking at it.

"G-U-E-S-T, you forget the 'U' Marta," Angelina replied, pointing to the spot on the sign with the missing letter and giving her beloved Marta a playful smile.

Marta looked over at Ben, "Sheesh! Ben, what does she want from me? I'm Polish!"

Ben's reply, as usual, was a little awkward. "You know Marta, there are two monuments in DC honoring Polish nationals who were instrumental in helping America gain its independence. General Thaddeus Kosciuszko, who helped win the battle of Saratoga, and Brigadier General Casimir Pulaski, who basically created America's first Cavalry!"

Marta's expression quickly went blank and she slowly turned to Angelina, "Does he always talk like that?"

Angelina laughed loudly, "Um, well...Yeah pretty much!"

Marta shook her head and declared, "Well then! I shall call you *Professor*! Well kids, you got your bags? Good, let's go meet the parents. Dum dum dummmm!"

Angelina laughed and grabbed Ben's hand wearing her always intoxicating smile. "They're going to love him, Marta! Stop it!"

As the trio closed in on the Rindge neighborhood, Ben was in awe of the beauty of the homes they were passing. The houses became more impressive as they drove and were spaced further apart as they approached their destination. Closely spaced, beautiful Colonial style houses gave way to vast estates with stunning landscaping that looked more like castles to Ben than single-family homes. When they finally pulled up to Angelina's parents' home in Wellesley, Massachusetts, Ben was speechless. The beautiful 9,500 square-foot home had a mix of stone and stained cedar shakes on the exterior, and was surrounded by meticulously groomed flower beds and manicured green lawns, multiple long cobblestone driveways, and walkways lined with stone walls. It was somehow not what Ben was expecting.

It was an early June evening, and the sun was already nearing the horizon. The New England air was much cooler than Ben was accustomed to for that time of year. The smell of freshly blossoming flowers and budding trees surrounding the property was powerful. Ben knew Angelina came from a wealthy family, but this was the most impressive house Ben had ever seen. As Ben stared at the flawless, dark-green lawn he wondered if anyone other than the person paid to care for it had ever stepped on it. Did anyone take time to enjoy the picture-perfect gardens with not so much as a flower petal out of place? His nerves had been calmed by the welcome and friendly nature of Marta, but they were acting up again. *What the hell am I doing here?*

"Professor Ben, my darling, we're here. What do you think? Will this be good enough for you?" Marta asked as she pulled into one of five garage doors around the backside of the stunning New England home.

"This is good enough for the fucking president," Ben mumbled under his breath. "Wow, Angelina, this place is amazing," Ben said with an awkward smile.

Mr. and Mrs. Rindge greeted the young couple as they walked into the house and Marta disappeared, leaving Ben looking around and wondering where she'd gone. Mr. Rindge was dressed casually in light khaki pants, blue dress shirt with no tie, and a brown-plaid sports jacket. He was several inches shorter than Ben, fit and tanned, with light brown hair combed to the side behind a receding hairline. He had a friendly face but spoke in short direct sentences like a man who was accustomed to getting what he wanted in a hurry.

"Mr. Gilsum, it's good to finally meet you," Mr. Rindge said to Ben with an extra firm handshake.

Ben tried to apply equal pressure but quickly decided that losing was the best way for him to win that battle. "Likewise, Mr. Rindge," Ben said as he eased his grip.

"Oh, enough of this mister business, you call him Bob at once Ben, and you can call me Deanne," Mrs. Rindge insisted as she pulled Ben to her with a hug that was far more warm and affectionate than any Ben had ever received prior. *Well, I guess she likes me!* That gave him the opportunity to notice that she wore the same perfume as her daughter, Joy by Jean Patou, which Ben enjoyed very much. Angelina didn't wear it often and Ben thought he might buy her some as a gift to encourage her to wear it more, but he would have never guessed it was among the costliest fragrances in the world, selling as high as $850 per ounce. Mrs. Rindge was positively lovely, tall like her daughter, taller than Mr. Rindge, with brown wavy hair cut a couple inches above her shoulders. She was elegant, full of class. She offered a smile when anyone looked in her direction. *My God, she looks like Jackie Kennedy!*

The presence of new faces belonging to his girlfriend's parents and the palatial surroundings sent the visibly uncomfortable Ben back to his shy and awkward shell, much to the disapproval of Angelina and especially her father. He was antsy, offering only short quiet answers to questions and staring in all directions other than into the eyes of the people he was talking to. The four spent the next hour talking about the flight to Boston, a brief and incomplete discussion about what Ben did for work and where he came from, and plans for the next two days before Ben and Angelina flew home Saturday evening. The plan was to give Ben his choice of activity for Friday afternoon. Anything he wanted to see in the Boston area was on the docket. But his response was met with confusion as none of the three knew what he was talking about.

"I'd really like to see a portion of the Henry Knox Trail," Ben said, showing enthusiasm for the first time in the conversation. "It should run just north of here and right into Boston."

The blank stares queued him to explain what he was talking about. "During the Revolutionary War, the British had captured Boston. George Washington gave orders to Henry Knox to bring guns from Fort Ticonderoga, which had been recently captured by the Americans, to Boston to help drive out the British. Henry Knox moved fifty-nine pieces of heavy artillery here from Upstate New York on frozen lakes and snowy trails. It was an amazing accomplishment!"

Mr. Rindge, who had considered himself a history buff, had never heard about any of this. His demeanor had changed from confusion to a man clearly impressed. Ben could tell he had won some respect from his pretty girlfriend's father and it felt nice. "OK campers, we're going to the Knox Trail on Friday! I just have to figure out where it is," Mr. Rindge announced as the young couple was shown to their room.

Ben had fully expected to be in a separate bedroom and intended to respect the Rindges' wishes, but to his surprise Mrs. Rindge had shown he and Angelina to one bedroom. "Goodnight, kids. Angel, it's positively heartwarming to have you home. Ben please feel welcome and make yourself at home," Mrs. Rindge said before another warm hug for both of her houseguests.

Chapter 21

Being in a strange place made it difficult for Ben to sleep. He was normally an early riser but woke up especially early his first morning at the Rindge home. He was able to reach his cellphone and check the time without disturbing Angelina who was sound asleep next to him in the king-sized bed in one of several spare bedrooms in the expansive New England home. *Not even six o'clock yet! What the hell am I gonna do for the next two hours!* Ben rolled over on his back and stared at the vaulted ceiling above him, thinking of how he would respond to the small talk he was dreading but fully expecting over the next couple of days. He'd rehearsed where he was from and what he did for work for the seventh time, since he was expecting more questions on those topics, when his phone began buzzing on the nightstand next to him. He'd received a text from an unknown sender, "Ben, it's Robert. If you're up come and join me in the sunroom for coffee." *You've got to be shitting me!*

The thought of pretending to be asleep crossed Ben's mind, but he knew he'd have a hard time lying that he'd not seen the text until after Angelina woke up. He took a deep breath, pulled himself together, and set out to find the sunroom.

"Ben, I'm over here," he heard as he was heading in the wrong direction from the kitchen, which was his only point of reference so far. "There you are. Angel told me you wake up pretty early like me. She gave me your number and suggested I text you at about six and save you from hours of boredom."

Did she!? I can't wait to thank her! Ben smiled and noticed there was a cup with black coffee in front of an empty chair in the sunroom.

"There's milk, sugar, Sweet and Low, however you like it."

Ben again smiled and sat in the chair set out for him; he pulled the warm cup closer for some comfort, "Black is perfect thank you, Mr. Rindge." Ben remained in retreat mode of his quiet and shy self only speaking when spoken to and wishing he could fast forward to when the women were awake. He could feel the contempt coming from his host, the same contempt he'd noticed most powerful figures felt for shy and awkward men. Especially those dating their youngest daughter.

Still, Mr. Rindge continued to smile at Ben and pretend to present a friendly demeanor, "So Ben, you're living pretty far north from Oklahoma. I can imagine DC took a bit of getting used to."

Ben was fully aware the mistake was intentional, "Actually I'm from Arkansas. I spend most of my time in Alexandria and around Mount Vernon, which is pretty rural, so it's not that much of an adjustment." *And the dreaded small talk begins.*

The two carried on for an hour and a half longer, which felt like an absolute eternity to Ben. There were never any real pressing questions and Ben was relieved to not explain what he did for work or what his life was like back home. Robert Rindge was a kind man and other than the intolerable shyness, he liked Ben. He had sized the young man up rather quickly and didn't believe he was right for Angelina. She was full of life, energy, and laughter. Ben would rather be somewhere else no matter where he was. Mr. Rindge had learned all he needed in the time it took Ben to finish his cup of coffee. The satisfied host sat quietly thinking to himself, *I'm not worried about my Angel at all. I'm actually worried about this poor, dumb bastard now.*

Things began to move rather quickly after the rest of the group was up. The foursome went into the city for the better part of the day. After a historic sightseeing cruise around Boston Harbor where they heard tales of the Revolutionary War and took in the nation's oldest continuously manned lighthouse, they had lunch at Faneuil Hall, which Mr. Rindge explained was the site of many speeches by Samuel Adams and other founding fathers. "This is the very place America began to take its shape politically. It's actually pretty exciting for me to be here."

Ben gave his typical smile though he knew exactly what Mr. Rindge meant and had often shared the same excitement around DC and other historic sites. He just failed to show that excitement today, much to his host's disappointment.

"OK, everyone, are we ready to go see the Henry Knox Trail?" Mr. Rindge asked the group.

Less than ten miles south of Faneuil Hall a small park in Roxbury, Massachusetts, is home of the first marker ever added to the Henry Knox Trail in 1926. A larger granite stone marker, similar in appearance to a gravestone, was added on March 27, 2009, dedicated by the Evacuation Day Heritage Committee; it reads, "THROUGH THIS PLACE PASSED THE NOBLE TRAIN OF ARTILLERY DELIVERED FROM FORT TICONDEROGA TO GENERAL GEORGE WASHINGTON BY MAJOR GENERAL HENRY KNOX AND PLACED AT DORCHESTER HEIGHTS BY JOHN THOMAS FORCING BOSTON'S FREEDOM AND THE EVACUATION OF BRITISH TROOPS ON MARCH 17, 1776." The scene around the modest monument was a small park with a few trees and trails. It was certainly not what one would consider a tourist attraction. The Rindge family now knew why they had never heard of the Henry Knox Trail.

"Well, this is exciting," Angelina said, poking fun at her boyfriend, who didn't immediately realize no one shared his enthusiasm.

Ben replied with a sheepish smile, "Well, it's no Faneuil Hall, is it?"

Mr. Rindge broke the awkward silence that followed, "OK, so we ready to head home?"

The ride home started out rather quietly. But Angelina could tell Ben was feeling a little embarrassed about dragging the family out to see a rock with a plaque on it so she quickly went to work to make him feel better. "So Ben. Baby. Are there any more tombstones in the middle of nowhere you'd like to see before we head back to DC?" Angelina said with a mischievous smile and a kiss before Ben could speak, not that he was about to utter anything more than a sheepish laugh.

The rest of the family gave a warmhearted chuckle and Mrs. Rindge replied, "Don't you worry about it, Ben. We all learned something interesting today. I'd never heard of Henry Knox before and the story was actually very interesting."

Mr. Rindge added with sarcasm that clearly showed from whom his lovely daughter inherited her personality. "Yeah, thanks for that Ben. I know I feel smarter now."

The young man from Arkansas just politely smiled and kept quiet for the rest of the way home, and for the rest of his time in Boston. Aside from his love of unusual historical facts, Benjamin Gilsum fit in among the high-class suburbanites of Boston about as much as anyone would expect a poor kid from an Arkansas chicken-farm town would. The fact was he never fit in back in Decatur, either. Back home, Ben was the kid who knew everything but could never really explain why. In high school, Ben's teachers would ask the class a question and make Ben wait until no one else could answer and then allow Ben to speak. Ben's answer was often followed by sighs from disgusted classmates.

Ben's love for memorizing got him into a bit of trouble as a junior in chemistry class. After reciting nearly the entire periodic table before the class Ben was awarded a fight with the defensive captain of the varsity football team. Ben could best be described as a difficult fit in any situation, which would explain why it was so hard for him to make and keep friends.

Ben's seemingly supernatural ability to read people also made matters exceedingly difficult for him in social situations. Knowing people were thinking negatively about him due to his quiet and awkward nature caused Ben to overcompensate, which highlighted his awkward nature even more. Most efforts to make people like him failed miserably. It would take Ben a long time to realize this and control it. It would take maturity and more time with Mr. James, who knew him more than he understood. It would take time for Ben to realize that knowing what people around you were feeling gave you no obligation to change it. Eventually, Ben would learn to allow people to change their feelings toward him naturally and ultimately accept him at their own pace.

Chapter 22

Ben was quiet with Angelina on the flight home from Boston. His visit did not go at all as planned and he was worried it had disappointed Angelina. The young couple was holding hands on the plane as Ben stared out the window lost in his anguish when Angelina broke the silence, "Baby, you need to snap out of it. I have great news for you that should cheer you up. Marta texted me before we got on the plane to tell me she adores you. She says you're too good for a spoiled brat like me, but I'm not supposed to tell you that part." Ben looked over at his pretty girlfriend's smiling face. *Good God, why is she with me?*

"Well, you know, she's absolutely right," Ben replied, "And I have a confession to make. When we land in DC, I'm going straight home to pack up my things and Marta and I are going to run off together!"

The mood between the young couple quickly returned to where it was before the trip to Boston, but Ben never stopped thinking he had lost some of the admiration Angelina had felt for him. Her bond with her father was strong, and it had been clear to everyone that Mr. Rindge was not impressed with Ben. He spent Saturday night tossing and turning unable to stop believing he had somehow lost the girl he was falling deeply in love with.

Ben felt sick about the trip to Boston, but not for long. As many young people do while falling in love, he stressed about every detail of his time with Angelina that didn't go exactly as he'd hoped it would. The anxiety lasted until they were together again and he realized she was over it. And Angelina was no different.

Angelina's feelings had grown just as strongly as Ben's. *I told my father about him! Took him home to be tortured by my daddy? What was I thinking? He must think I'm a psycho!* The beautiful young woman from Boston who broke through Ben's reluctance to let go and enjoy himself loved witnessing his transformation. Sometimes when he was cutting loose, she would stop and watch him enjoying the moment. She would stare in awe at the new man she helped create and be overcome with emotion. *Wait! Holy shit what am I doing? I'm actually falling for this guy!*

Chapter 23

I t was a struggle to get out of bed Sunday morning in time to be ready for Mr. James. As Mr. James had asked him to, Ben had gone over everything they spoke about during their last visit. Ben couldn't help but wonder where the story was going and if he had made a mistake trying to join a religious organization. Ben believed in something he considered God, but he wasn't sure about much of the rest. He remembered that Mr. James had told him to form his own opinion but to pay attention to the stories and be ready to discuss at his petition for initiation. Ben would continue cautiously with that in mind.

The always punctual Mr. James showed up exactly on time, with the same unwavering and pleasant demeanor; he was wearing wool slacks with sneakers and a sweater. Ben couldn't help but like the old man. He was happy and kind every time they met. He seemed so excited to visit with Ben and had repeated several times that his work with Ben made him feel as though he was getting younger and full of energy himself.

"Ben, let's get right into it my son." It was the first of many times Mr. James would call him son. Ben wasn't comfortable with it in the beginning, as he was fiercely loyal to his parents, but in time it grew on him and he eventually learned to like it.

"We left off with the basic formation of Satan and Hell, with a brief set of rules between Hell and Earth."

Ben nodded to confirm that he remembered.

"Well Ben, that's when things get really interesting. You now have three characters, if you will, to the story. There is God, the devil, and man. Now, the relationship between the three remained constant for many years, centuries even. God showered love on man, man continued to prove to be human and to sin, often punished by God but always loved and always granted passage to the Kingdom of Heaven upon death. And Satan grew more and more angry, tempting man as often as he could to prove to God that man was not worthy of such a gift. It was in God's punishment of living man for his sins on Earth that Satan would see his opportunity. Satan knew man was growing weary of being punished by God. Through temptation from Satan, man would cry out to God in anger. Man wanted the punishment on Earth to stop. Man wanted God to stop interfering with the living."

Mr. James stopped to check on his young friend, "Ben, this may feel like a sermon, but it's important. How are you doing?"

Ben responded rather positively, to his delight, "Actually, this is beginning to get interesting, I'm still with you."

Mr. James continued, "Very well then, I'll try to keep it as painless as possible and stick to the point. God granted man his wish, but there would be an enormous price that to this day man may not fully appreciate. Man would be allowed to rule Earth alone, without God's physical presence and without earthly punishment for his sin. In exchange for such remarkable autonomy, man would have to show his worthiness on Earth before being granted passage into the Kingdom of Heaven upon death. Failure to prove worthiness would result in banishment to Hell with Satan and the demon angels forever. This is a very important moment in the history of humankind, Ben. It was at this moment that God bestowed upon man his greatest yet most dangerous gift. God granted man free will on Earth. With that agreement, God left Earth with a promise to return in human form so he may enter and leave Earth in the same manner that man does. Once God leaves Earth in human form, the agreement is sealed and he will never return, leaving man to rule the Earth and prove he is worthy before rejoining God in the Kingdom of Heaven. Such a remarkable yet terrifying gift to bestow on humans. Satan rejoiced in God's decision as he believed this would be the beginning of man's undoing forever."

Mr. James could tell that Ben's mind was wandering and there was still so much to discuss, so he made a decision to end the lesson there and pick up in a week during their next Sunday visit. He changed the topic with what little time the two had left to their scheduled session. "Ben, I want to stop there and spend a little time talking about something else if you don't mind."

This would become the normal process from that point forward when the two men got together. Mr. James would discuss what Ben needed to know for his initiation into the Brothers, and then he would become more of a personal mentor and discuss how Ben could better control what he would eventually understand to be his gifts. At first, these personal discussions were uncomfortable for Ben; he couldn't see what the old man was talking about and it felt awkward. Ben's father was an excellent example to follow for moral standards and a terrific source for practical knowledge, but was simply not available for talking about feelings or emotions and how they affected a person's behavior. Ben's discussions with Mr. James helped him open up and not just with people close to him. The knowledge and self-awareness that Mr. James was offering to Ben enabled him to interact more personably with people that were not emotionally close to him. Over time, as Ben saw improvements in his own social life, he recognized it was the direct result of considering what Mr. James was telling him. His trust in his friend grew. Ben treasured the advice and knowledge Mr. James was sharing with him because when he listened his life improved.

Ben would come to realize that Mr. James shared the same gifts he had, and this understanding began a bond between the two men that would last for the rest of Ben's life. Ben had never met a person who understood why he could read people so well, know if they were trustworthy, and why he sometimes knew immediately when someone was telling the truth. More critically, Mr. James understood why there were a few Ben could not read at all. He had assumed Ted shared the same ability, but he was never certain and the two never discussed it. Ben learned a lot more from Mr. James than just the lore of the Brothers of Herrad. Ben learned how to live with his abilities and how to control them without hiding from them and the rest of the world.

Chapter 24

With his lesson concluded for the day, Ben was planning to spend the rest of Sunday relaxing and doing next to nothing when he received an unusual visit from his landlord. Ben was always prompt in dealing with the business between the two and the only time the two men talked otherwise was while Ben was helping with various projects around the property. Both men kept to themselves most of the time.

"Hello, Ben, pardon the interruption but I noticed you've had a frequent visitor," his landlord said.

Ben smiled, "Yeah, that's my girlfriend Angel. She's…"

Ben was interrupted, "No not her, she's really pretty by the way, Ben. I was talking about the man that was here this morning."

Ben laughed, "Oh, that's Mr. James. He'll be coming here for a few more Sundays. He's working with me…"

Ben was interrupted again, "That's Jim Tamworth. He's a good man, I used to know him before I retired."

Ben looked stunned. The landlord continued, "I also noticed Jim had a younger man with him a few weeks ago. Bill Sullivan, I believe. I knew his father. I used to work with him when I was active." *Active? What do you mean active?* "The father's name is Bradford Sullivan. Brad and I worked together on several projects before I retired. If I'm not mistaken, he's still working and still active." *What the hell does active mean?*

"Ben, Bill's father is into some pretty serious stuff around Washington, DC. He goes by the name of Mr. White, or at least he used to."

The smile on Ben's face quickly dropped and his mind began to race. *Are you kidding me? Could he mean…*

"Ben, you're a great kid and the best tenant I could have hoped for. Who you have over for company is your business. I'm not going to tell you who to associate with, that's not why I'm here."

Ben's face remained blank and his landlord knew Ben knew of Mr. White.

"Ben, the Sullivans have a great deal of influence and power. I'm not so sure it's good influence either. I knew Mr. White very well from my younger years. Ben, just be careful, that's why I barged in on you this morning. I want you to be careful. A good kid like you might stay clear of people like the Sullivans."

The expression on Ben's face never changed, even after his landlord left him to his Sunday morning alone. He was positively numb and wasn't sure what to think about what he was just told. Ben never really got to know his landlord beyond the fact he was a nice old man who gave him a fantastic deal on a terrific apartment in the woods. He was kind and quiet, and appreciated having a young man around to help keep his beloved old place looking nice. Ben would never know Bryan Ashland, AKA Mr. Black, once worked very closely with Bradford Sullivan, AKA Mr. White, when he was "active." Back then the two men specialized in acquiring weapons and sending them discreetly to places in the world that the U.S. Government either wanted to assist privately or sometimes did not want to assist at all but needed to offer something in exchange for a deal that most Americans knew nothing about. Mr. Black had retired a relatively wealthy man several years before he met Ben and was living out his life without ever being implicated in any scandal.

Chapter 25

Thankfully, Ben was busy at work Monday morning. It had been an exceptionally long weekend, and he had a heavy load of complicated things on his mind. He needed something to keep him focused. He needed something to prevent him from doing what was inevitable. He had logged several hours researching the Brothers of Herrad already at work. He suspected he could "follow up" again without raising suspicion, but there was a twist now that he never considered before. Bradford Sullivan's son was an officer with the group. Bradford Sullivan was Mr. White. Ben had never heard of anyone in his position knowing the actual name of one of their contacts at the federal government. Surely any searches into his government contact's family would be discovered and grounds for immediate termination and perhaps even legal charges. But Jim Tamworth was an unknown. Ben could look into Mr. James and his activities and learn more about the Brothers without getting too close to Mr. White. Ben would have to resist the temptation to look into Bryan Ashland, but he would leave that well enough alone.

Ben returned to his desk after lunch with little to do. He sat in his small, six feet by eight feet office looking at the blank, white wall in front of him.

Ben was proud of the fact that he had an actual office and not a cubicle like everyone in the company who was fresh out of college, although there was barely room for his desk. There was no window in Ben's office. It was located in the interior of the seven-story square building, which was a dull, concrete box with only a few narrow windows to the outside. The building was kept clean and neat, never so much as a stray piece of paper in sight, partly because many of the documents in the building were classified. The building's interior was as dull as the exterior with very little decoration or plants of any kind. The work that people were doing was expected to be completely void of personal opinion or expression and the physical environment inside the building reflected that expectation. It was always cold. The air conditioner seemed to run constantly and most of the employees looked dressed for winter, even on hot Virginia summer days. It was normally quiet, eerily quiet in most of the building, except for the cafeteria area where people ate their lunch and made their coffee. Except for his regular conversations with Ted, Ben kept mostly to himself and the environment at the company suited him fine.

Ben's office had three plain, white walls and a fourth facing the hallway; it had a glass door with two glass panels on either side. Ben and his coworkers referred to their part of the building as the exhibit because the little offices with one glass wall reminded them of a museum. Most people working in the exhibit area chose to situate their desk facing out toward the glass wall, allowing privacy for whatever it was they were working on or perhaps not working at all on. Ben faced sideways in his office and was not concerned about his coworkers seeing his computer screen. The young intelligence analyst felt more comfortable not exchanging stares with people in the hallway passing by and he knew that no one cared about what he was working on or looking at in his office. They simply moved on and minded their business. One morning Ben arrived at his office to find a member of maintenance installing a shade over the glass panel that was on the side where Ben kept his chair. Ben never questioned who requested it or why. He was happy that he didn't have to move his desk.

His small office was impeccable. Everything on Ben's desk had its place and was immediately returned after use. The three white walls were bare except for a framed print of the signing of the Declaration of Independence by French artist Charles Edouard Armand-Dumaresq, which hung on the wall behind him. The painting was Ben's favorite depiction of the signing because he liked how it portrayed the room the colonial leaders assembled in at the Pennsylvania State House, now known as Independence Hall. That room was simple and modestly decorated where other versions tended to dress the room up more than the young history enthusiast felt was authentic.

Having spare time in the afternoon was a common pattern for the young man. Ben liked to be busy and when he had work to do he was focused and efficient. He would work hard in the morning, getting all of his daily tasks done before lunchtime. This would allow him to jump right into any new activity in the afternoon without delay, which always impressed his superiors. He could then go home with an empty desk. Ben hated to leave the office with unfinished work. This habit would sometimes leave Ben with little to do for the second half of his workday. Now Ben was experiencing one of those afternoons so he gave in to the inevitable and decided a "follow up" on the Brothers of Herrad was in order. Just like in sixth grade social studies, he had to finish the lesson! *I need to know more about these guys.* He began looking into the activities and communications of the group's most senior members. Ben began researching James Tamworth.

The most interesting information about Mr. James was he was ninety-eight years old, still had a driver's license, and lived alone. He was a widower with two daughters, one had passed away, four grandchildren, seven great-grandchildren and even a great-great-grandchild named Brooklyn. Mr. James had never been in any trouble with the law. In fact, he had a perfect driving record without so much as a speeding ticket anywhere on file. He was president and owner of several banks and retired before turning sixty. Mr. James had made many wise investments and was far wealthier than Ben had imagined. There were more charitable connections than Ben could count, mostly to children's causes. It seemed that Mr. James did very little communicating electronically, which Ben should have suspected from a man nearly a century old. Mr. James was exactly as he had presented himself to be. He was a kind-hearted older gentleman who enjoyed helping others, and he spent nearly all of his time and a staggering amount of money doing just that. Ben could find no connections to William or Bradford Sullivan, which meant virtually all of their communication was in person or in written form. This search ended just like all other prior searches into the activity of the Brothers of Herrad. *These guys really are saints!*

There was still an hour left to Ben's workday when he finished with his research on Mr. James. He would spend the entire hour staring at a blank screen with a blinking cursor next to the name William Sullivan. Ben did not press Enter, at least not today.

Chapter 26

Ben managed to avoid temptation and trouble at work the entire week; on Thursday, his usual stop at the Columbia Firehouse was spent alone. Angelina was busy with some projects at work so he would dine at a high-top table near the bar by himself. As usual, when he was alone he spoke to no one and casually observed the people around him, offering a smile to anyone who made eye contact.

Ben had finished his dinner and was about to order a second draft when the waitress ignored his request and instead took a seat across from him at his table. She paused a while, waiting for Ben to say something, staring at him with her striking green eyes. She soon realized that he wouldn't budge and the two would only become increasingly uncomfortable. She was petite, pretty, with long red hair she pulled back into a ponytail. Her cheeks were a little flush due to the activity around the bar, but mostly due to her fair skin. Things around the bar were busy but Ben was her only customer for the moment. Patty had been trying for months to get the quiet young man to notice her but had failed and was now conceding to the much more aggressive Angelina Rindge.

"I just wanted to let you know how happy I am for you," she said with a lovely smile.

Ben smiled in return but he was obviously confused.

"Angelina had been asking about you for weeks and I finally told her everything I knew, which I'm afraid was barely more than your name. Anyway, I'm sure you don't mind that I told her. You two are great together and all of us here are so glad you're happy. She seems to bring out the best in you, Ben. I really love to see it."

A customer interrupted, "Patty, could I have another bay breeze when you get a chance cutie pie?"

Patty replied, "Absolutely, Claire, on my way," to an older woman a few tables over, who looked like she didn't need another bay breeze.

So that's Patty! Ben had seen her a hundred times but never really paid much attention. He never realized how pretty she was or how deep a crush she had on him. Ben could feel a mix of joy and pain from Patty as she again said how happy she was for him and Angelina before retreating from his table to track down a bay breeze for her thirsty patron. She touched his hand and gave him one last smile with sad eyes before leaving him alone. Ben was a little stricken by Patty. How had he not noticed her before now? He could see beyond any doubt that she was attracted to him and though she smiled and declared her happiness for him, he knew she was hurting inside. Ben drifted a little deeper in thought, then quickly stopped himself. He was falling in love with someone else who was perhaps the most incredible person he had ever met. *What the hell am I doing?* Ben decided not to order a second beer and left enough cash to cover his bill and a generous tip on the table for Patty.

Chapter 27

When Sunday came around Ben started the morning early, setting out coffee and donuts for Mr. James. He had been looking forward to his visit. Ben had been thinking of ways to ask his old friend more about Billy and somehow confirm his connection to Bradford Sullivan, who Ben had come to know as Mr. White. The news that Mr. White was Billy Sullivan's father was positively stunning to Ben, and he still wasn't sure if he believed it. He had to be very careful about saying "Mr. White" when referring to Billy or his father, whoever that may actually be.

Ben was content to ignore all the warnings about the Brothers and continue to proceed with his Sunday study sessions. He had yet to confirm anything negative about the group using highly sophisticated methods. He'd actually only discovered the contrary and the mystery around the group and its members were becoming even more intriguing. Ben still maintained that at any point he was free to leave the group, and Mr. James had given him no reason to think otherwise.

The old man arrived exactly on time and greeted his star pupil with a typical feeble handshake and smile and wearing his usual wool trousers with sneakers and a sweater. Ben sensed a little trepidation in his friend.

Mr. James noticed the coffee and donuts, but as usual, asked for a glass of water.

"Would you like some coffee? I got us some donuts, too," Ben said.

"No, thank you, Ben. I stopped drinking coffee before you were born. Caffeine is not your friend, my son. And if I eat one of those, I'll spend the afternoon feeling like I ingested a brick. Water is fine, Ben."

Ben got his friend a glass of water as requested, "Is everything OK, Mr. James?" Ben asked, not able to ignore that his friend was upset about something.

"Oh yes, everything is fine. I do need to inform you that we'll have just one more session after today though. It seems the Worshipful Master of our order is anxious to make you a member, Ben. No worry, we can speed things up and have you ready for initiation, though I wish you and I had more time together."

Ben was excited about the news, "Mr. James, you and I can still spend time together when all of this is over. Can't we?"

The old man was visibly moved by Ben's question, "Of course we can, Ben, that would be very nice."

Ben could sense there was something Mr. James wasn't telling him. *Is he not feeling well? Don't tell me you're about to retire completely from the Brothers!* Ben hoped he would learn more during this visit.

"Don't worry, Ben, I'm not going to leave you any time soon," Mr. James said with a chuckle. "And just for the record son, I've told the rest of the Brothers I refuse to die until you become an officer with the order!"

Ben was relieved to hear the words his old friend spoke, answering his concerns without the need to ask. The two often communicated as if they could read one another's mind, and questions were often answered that were never asked out loud.

"We left off with the agreement in place that God would allow man to rule on Earth without interference. Things are going to get a bit strange now, Ben, as we stray far from what you may have learned in church or Sunday school," Mr. James added to be sure his young friend was paying attention. "You know the story of Jesus' birth on Earth as the son of God and as God himself in some religions. I'm sure you're also aware of the three wise men that traveled from strange lands to witness the birth of Jesus. You may not know who those three wise men or kings were according to our order and the secret writings of Herrad. Son, those three kings were a representation of the three parties involved in this agreement set between God and man which was ultimately put into motion by Satan. The first king represented God, the second Satan, and the third king was there to witness for man."

"The first king was named Patisar. He left the gift of myrrh, which was used in those times for medicinal purposes and also as a perfume to ease the smell of death and disease. The second king was named Caspar. He left the gift of gold, likely a temptation. The third king is of particular importance to our group and to all of humankind for that matter. The third king embodied representation for man and was named Melchior. In ancient Hebrew, Melchior translates to 'King of Light.' His gift was frankincense. Frankincense was produced from tree sap and in those times used for medicinal purposes. It was known as the healing oil of the Earth."

Ben was looking skeptical of all of this and couldn't hide his feelings. *So the three wise men at the manger were what, lawyers!?*

Mr. James stopped a moment and smiled. "Now, Ben, remember, all of this is open to interpretation. We may never know if any of this is actually true, but there's something we can take away from the overall message of the writings and teachings. No one is asking or even expecting us to believe all of this literally. The important thing for the Brothers of Herrad is that we live our lives in a way that shows we are open to proving ourselves and mankind worthy of God's love..."

Mr. James continued and Ben drifted away, not paying attention. *Great, here comes another sermon!*

"...We require that you remain open to these teachings and make an effort to abide by them."

"I understand, Mr. James," Ben offered politely and tried better to hide his doubts and his boredom.

"Very well, son. We're almost done with today's lesson and I think what we don't go over today will be finished up quite nicely next Sunday. All that was left after the three kings witnessed and confirmed the birth of Christ was for God to live among man and die, leaving Earth in the same manner as humankind…"

Ben lost focus again, *I wonder what Angel is up to.* As he came back from his daydream Mr. James was still going,

"…We believe all who live an honorable life based on God's teachings are worthy of the Kingdom of Heaven. That's an important distinction of the Brothers of Herrad. Upon the confirmation that God had taken human form, the three kings left and vanished forever. The agreement was sealed upon the death of Jesus Christ. God shall never return to Earth, leaving mankind to rule and control his own destiny with his own free will."

Mr. James could tell he hadn't completely sold Ben on the teachings of the Brothers of Herrad, but the young man was considering what he said about remaining open to living his life according to the principle of the writings.

"Ben, I think we'll stop there today," Mr. James said.

The old man remained a short time to talk with Ben as he did every Sunday about matters not related to the Brothers of Herrad. This was the part of the visits that Ben now treasured. In these moments with Mr. James, Ben was gaining an understanding of himself and why he behaved in the manner he did. Ben realized why he was so shy, distant, and not willing to engage with strangers. Mr. James made Ben understand himself and that understanding was making Ben more capable of interacting with the world around him. His old friend was helping him to create a strong desire to be more a part of his surroundings and not just exist as a silent observer. Mr. James was saving Ben from a life in solitude and the more time Ben spent with Mr. James, the more he would come to understand the value of that.

Chapter 28

T hings had been slow at work for weeks with few exceptions. In part, it was because there weren't a lot of requests from the government, but more so because Ben was increasingly efficient at completing his assignments. Ben once again finished all of his tasks before lunch, leaving little to do but daydream. He had also become proficient at being creative with logging his activity without there being any actual activity. Ben still dreaded having nothing to do. It had occurred to him he had performed several unauthorized searches without raising suspicion or having to answer any questions. He simply updated his activity log that he was following up on the activities and communications of the Brothers of Herrad, which was requested of him several weeks earlier. Now he had information he obtained lawfully that he did not have before. He had the name of an officer of the group, William Sullivan, and had been informed that he was a Senior Deacon. Ben had convinced himself that what he was about to do was perfectly lawful and dutiful even. The fact that there was a personal motive was purely a coincidence.

William Sullivan was actually from Boston and had an MBA from a fine New England college. He was an independent executive consultant who had connections to some well-known corporate officers in a variety of industries. There was so much information to process that Ben considered letting it go so he didn't spend too much time working on something he had only half-heartedly convinced himself was morally acceptable. He determined he would minimize his efforts to anything related to the Brothers of Herrad, but that limitation eliminated all material. Just like before there was nothing about the Brothers of Herrad on record.

Ben narrowed his search to communications with one particular CEO and went from there. He picked one at random and proceeded, then another and the same. He repeated this process several times and made an astonishing discovery. William Sullivan was not communicating with these people about ideas to help their corporations run more efficiently. There was nothing about streamlining processes, improving efficiency, consolidating locations, training, hiring, firing, or capital investment. In fact, there was nothing about advising anyone on how to improve a company, nor anything about individual motivation techniques, or self-improvement methods. Ben found communications about meeting in private to discuss legal matters but Billy was definitely not a lawyer. Social engagements were often discussed followed by very large charitable contributions to an undisclosed organization. Every communication had the same theme and ended in the same manner. The corporate officer was doing something they wanted to be kept secret, and every one of them discussed with Billy both a fee for his services and a "substantial contribution to an undisclosed charitable organization." *What the heck is Billy up to!?*

Ben was overwhelmed with the information he uncovered and was left with a partially solved mystery. He knew Billy was keeping illegal or immoral activity a secret for a fee and a donation to the Brothers of Herrad, but he didn't know how. How was Billy able to keep these secrets hidden? What connection did Billy have...*OH NO!!!* It didn't take long for Ben to find the answer which he felt should have been more obvious to him. *These dirty deeds aren't being hidden from law enforcement, they're just being completely ignored or hidden from the inside once they get there!* When he discovered the link to Bradford Sullivan, who unknown to the public also worked in federal law enforcement as an agent known as Mr. White, Ben decided it best to conclude his search. He shut down his computer and left his office to go outside for some fresh air. Ben sat outside and for a moment thought about not going back into the building. *How can this be happening? Where do I go from here!?*

"Hey, young fella, what are you doing out here? You're not a smoker. Are you?" Ted asked.

Ben spun around and saw his boss approaching him with a smile and an unlit cigarette hanging from his lip. *Oh shit!* "I just needed some fresh air," Ben said nervously. *He knows something is up, he knows!*

Ted looked at his obviously uneasy subordinate and put his hand on his shoulder, "Ben, son, whatever worry is on your mind, let it go. You're too young and too damn handsome to be so nervous. A young man like you shouldn't worry about anything for too long my friend." Ted chuckled before lighting up his cigarette, "Oh damn, sorry to foul up your fresh air," Ted added as he waved away his initial puff of smoke.

Chapter 29

I t was Sunday morning and Ben welcomed his friend and mentor, who was perfectly punctual as usual, to his home for the last time. This time, Ben's mind was full of doubt, fear, and trepidation. Mr. James, wearing his customary wool trousers with sneakers and a sweater, and happily accepting his typical glass of water, immediately sensed his friend was troubled but offered an unusually brief bit of advice, "Ben, whatever it is, trust yourself and you'll be fine. You're a good man son, believe that. God knows I do. Trust yourself and spend your life earning that trust."

The younger man had agonized for days about what he learned from reading communication involving Billy and potentially Bradford Sullivan. Ben knew there had to be a person either inside the federal government or worse at the company working in cooperation with Billy to shield his corporate clients. To this point there was no link back to Mr. James and Ben still believed his friend was a virtuous man, and a great man. He had seen much of the good work the Brothers were doing all over Alexandria and beyond. Ben's time with his mentor had improved his understanding of himself and given him the confidence he could improve his own life beyond his prior expectations. Still, Ben was more apprehensive than ever about joining the Brothers of Herrad. Yet, he didn't want to stop now. He wanted to learn more. He wanted to prove to himself that Mr. James was the man he thought he was, and he didn't want to disappoint his old friend. Ben would take the old man's advice and trust himself.

"Today we're going to focus on what happened after God left Earth forever and humankind was left to rule themselves on Earth with the promise of eternity in the Kingdom of Heaven should they prove worthy," Mr. James began. "After the death of Christ, for roughly a thousand years, mankind appeared to be lost and unworthy. The temptations from Lucifer were impossible to resist. However, it was after a thousand years that a group of men from Europe, you may know them as Crusaders, found the very teachings we're discussing today in present-day Israel. These men formed a fellowship and later came to be known as the Knights Templar. I'll allow you to read up on their remarkable history and legend on your own time. There's plenty there to keep you busy if you choose."

"These men had become quite powerful as I'm sure you're aware and shared much of their knowledge with the world, but they didn't share all of it. After the Knights Templar were betrayed by the Church and nearly wiped out, most of what was left of them gathered their wealth and fled to modern day Switzerland to become farmers and give rise to a new and oddly powerful nation. Odd because that collection of farmers produced one of the most elite fighting forces in Europe along with a notoriously secure banking system. For hundreds of years, no one understood why until the connection to the Knights Templar was revealed. The few Knights who remained in France and England held on to a smaller share of wealth, but a far greater share of texts and teachings. These men continued their bond and according to legend, formed a private society you very well may have heard of. The group, legends say, is now known as the Freemasons."

Ben perked up, "Really? I'd heard rumors that the Freemasons were remnants of Knights Templar. So are the Brothers of Herrad Freemasons then?"

Mr. James gave his usual smile and answered, "We'll get there, Ben. We'll get there. I'm glad you're still awake son."

"The Freemasons were known to be dedicated to enlightenment and improving all of humankind by first reaching their own full potential. Many believe by witnessing the good deeds and respect for their fellow man, people would respond by following the example set by the group and society would be better for it. It's been said the Freemasons determined that the knowledge they obtained was best kept secret and improving society was in order before sharing of that knowledge would be appropriate. This group thrived in Europe for five hundred years when a unique opportunity to change the world presented itself. I'm referring, of course, to the discovery of the New World. Vast amounts of untamed land and other resources an ocean away from Europe. An opportunity they would seize upon and eventually create a remarkable new nation. As I'm sure you're aware, there were many Freemasons among our founding fathers. Their principles and ideology are sprinkled all over the Declaration of Independence and Constitution. These concepts were fresh and new and quickly gobbled up by most of the civilized world. It was a momentous achievement and legend has it that many among the Freemasons believed it was time to share all the knowledge they held secret for so many years. However, the leadership of the group felt there was still work to be done."

"Over the many years that followed there have been dark moments in our nation's history that may very well have proven we still aren't quite ready for enlightenment. Some would argue sharing knowledge could have prevented many of those dark moments. Still, the debate rages on among the so called secret society. One bit of that knowledge rumored to be held by Freemasons was the secret writings of Herrad of Landsberg. You remember her? She's the creator of Hortus Deliciarum; we spoke about her during our first session."

Ben nodded and Mr. James continued, "A leader among the Freemasons was fascinated by the very teachings we've been talking about for weeks. He wanted to focus more on this information, but the rest of the leadership had apparently long forgotten those teachings or had gone as far as rejecting them completely. After a lengthy discussion, this very powerful member of the group was given permission to leave, taking a couple of items with him."

"The departing member took with him the secret writings of Herrad of Landsberg and with that text, he formed his own group. He had to promise two things in exchange for leaving with the writings. First, he would work in the same manner as the Freemasons, with the same goal to improve society in the hope of helping humankind become worthy of enlightenment. And second, he would not reveal any of the knowledge he had obtained including the documents he left with to society until the Freemasons had done the same with their vast wealth of knowledge. He agreed and quickly formed the Brothers of Herrad. We have many of the same traditions as the Freemasons, but only two relics. The first, of course, is the writings from Herrad of Landsberg that we've been discussing, and the second is an ancient ring worn by the Worshipful Master or chosen leader of our group. This ring represents our allegiance to Melchior, the third king and representative of mankind who was present at the birth of Jesus Christ."

"That's it, my young friend!" Mr. James nearly shouted as he noticed Ben had gone glossy eyed.

"So, the Brothers of Herrad are actually a spinoff of the Freemasons?" Ben asked.

"Well, I suppose you could look at it that way, Ben. We're not nearly as rigid as them, though. You won't have to memorize texts written in a strange code and recite them later for advancement or anything like that, and we don't have various degrees or levels the way the Freemasons do. We have officers with titles that are the same as the Freemasons, and we require our members to believe in God as they do. Beyond those similarities, you'll find our group to be quite different. I would even encourage you to seek membership with the Freemasons if you're curious. You can join both groups."

No thanks! "I think I'll stick to one secret society," Ben replied.

"Private society," Mr. James responded.

"Our work here is done," Mr. James announced, "You've been an excellent pupil, my son. I hope you've found our discussions interesting. I suspect we'll be in touch quickly to have you come to the lodge and complete your petition for initiation. You'll be asked questions about our discussions and be expected to have more than a basic understanding of them. If your answers satisfy our members, your petition will be accepted. There's a ceremonial proceeding followed by your oath to not share what you've learned with anyone outside the group."

Mr. James stood, indicating he was ready to leave and Ben stood with him and walked him to the door. Before walking out Mr. James paused, staring at his young friend, "Ben, I can't express how excited I am to have you join us. I meant what I said before, son. You're a good man, and you'll make a fine officer one day."

Ben shook the old man's outstretched hand and offered a smile and quiet 'thank you' in response. Ben was never very comfortable accepting compliments.

Chapter 30

Sitting across from Angelina at their favorite high-top table at the Firehouse Thursday night, Ben's mind was wandering, and he was barely listening to his beautiful girlfriend telling him all about her crazy day. The bar was unusually busy for a Thursday, with patrons and staff buzzing all about. It was the Thursday before the Fourth of July weekend and Alexandria was loaded with tourists from all around the country. Angelina was practically shouting over the noise, but Ben appeared to be tuning both it and her out. Ben's thoughts were elsewhere. He had paused his personal investigation into the members of the Brothers after his odd run-in with Ted had shaken him. He also decided to keep going forward with his initiation and once a member, he would decide what to do about Billy. *Trust yourself.* Mr. James' words echoed in Ben's mind. Ben trusted Mr. James completely. And he knew it was not only important to trust himself, it was equally important that he earn that trust and honor it as he would the trust of another person. He would work for the rest of his life to earn his own trust, as Mr. James suggested. *I can't stop now, I need to learn more. Trust yourself.*

"Babe? Are you listening?" Angelina said waving her hand in front of Ben's eyes.

"Yeah, sorry it's been insane this past couple of weeks. Work stuff and you know, my meetings with Mr. James and initiation," Ben answered.

"Ooh, yea!" Angelina replied, "I think what you're doing is awesome babe. You have so much potential and the people you're gonna meet there can open up some great opportunities for you. You'd be amazed what knowing the right people can do for you in this town!"

Ben felt something he'd never experienced before with Angelina. She was not being sincere. Her words were encouraging and supportive but there was something else and Ben couldn't quite figure it out. She wasn't lying and her passion perked up when she went on about how much the Freemasons did for her father. Still, Ben sensed something wasn't right.

"So anyway, babe, go for it! This could totally change your life. I'm excited for you!" Angelina said with her beautiful smile.

No, she isn't, why?

"How's my favorite couple?" Patty shouted, taking the young lovers by surprise. "Oh, and for the record, the two hottest people in the place!" Patty added, looking around, pretending she was checking out the competition, "Not even close!"

Ben lit up, and his pretty girlfriend noticed immediately. "Hey, Patty, how've you been? Great to see you," Ben shouted.

Ben and Patty exchanged an extended stare and enthusiastic smile. "I'm doing well, Ben, and hey good luck with your initiation. That's pretty exciting, huh?" Patty added a quick goodbye to Angelina as she left the table and got back to work.

Angelina's lovely and seemingly perpetual smile was gone as she looked at her young boyfriend with her eyebrows raised and her head tilted downward and toward the right side, "Oh, really? Been hangin with Patty, have ya, honey?"

Though she was clearly bothered and there was no hiding that from Ben, her tone quickly returned to pleasant and she let out a laugh that wasn't fully sincere, "Listen up, Tiger! If you wanna know what's best, I'd avoid spending too much time with the waitress, ya know what I'm sayin? I'm fully capable of taking a nine iron to that pretty face of yours!"

Ben took a few seconds before speaking, unsure how to respond.

"Don't worry, babe! I'm only kidding," Angelina lied, laughing. "If you could see your face! I love Patty, she's awesome. She's also kinda hot, I mean if you're into that sort of thing, maybe we could work out a three-way."

Ben half-heartedly laughed and when his mind was done digesting what Angelina had just said about a three-way, he gave his girlfriend most of his attention the rest of the night. Yet, he couldn't help but wonder about the mixed feelings he had picked up on. Something had changed in Angelina; Ben sensed it was more than just petty jealousy. He had never picked up on it before, but he was convinced it wasn't new. Ben was gifted at sensing a person's sincerity and emotion, and since he had spent his entire life suppressing his own emotions, he automatically attributed anything he was feeling to others. This was something he and Mr. James had discussed. Mr. James had warned him of this and Ben was now recognizing the truth in his old friend's advice. Now Ben was stuck wondering, had the jubilation and admiration he sensed in Angelina mostly belonged to him? Had his feelings faded some and allowed him to get a better sense of hers? Feelings that now seemed mixed? Ben shrugged it off and considered the fact that he was experiencing a great deal of stress at the moment. There was no point in making assumptions and he was determined to stick to the things he knew. Angelina was very good to Ben. She was also very good for him, and he knew it. *I better get the hell outta my head or I'm gonna lose this girl!*

Chapter 31

t was the night of the petition for initiation at the Brothers. Ben was sitting alone in his Jeep Wrangler, dressed in a suit and parked on the street near the modest building he had once checked out from the outside. It was hot and Ben was uncomfortable in his suit and tie. Sweat was beginning to build on his forehead, but he didn't want to run his Jeep just to turn on the air conditioning. He was early, fidgeting with his tie and waiting for seven o'clock, the scheduled time for his petition. He could see from where he was parked just a short distance away and across the street that there was a great deal of activity in the building this time. He had noticed several exceptionally well-dressed men of all ages entering the building. Ben was nervous but not because he didn't remember everything he and Mr. James talked about in preparation for this moment. That part was easy. He was nervous because he was thinking of the various warnings he had received from Ted, his landlord Mr. Ashland, and by his own secret research into the activities of Billy Sullivan. *Should I be doing this?*

A faint tapping on his car window interrupted the young initiate's thoughts. He looked up and saw his mentor standing on the sidewalk with Billy Sullivan holding his other arm as he was leaning over to get Ben's attention. "No shame in being early, son, why don't you come on in with me and we'll get started? My Brothers have all arrived and are eager to meet you," Mr. James said as he stood up straight, relieving Billy of his duties to hold him up.

"It's nice to see you again, Benjamin," Billy said as he left Mr. James' side and indicated by pointing to the door that he was heading in. *Ugh, Benjamin!?*

"You as well, Billy, and please just call me Ben," Ben replied to Billy's back as he was already opening the door of the building and entering alone.

"We're going to stop in the lobby and make preparations before going into the main hall," Mr. James said as Ben stepped out of his car. "I'm afraid you'll have to wear a blindfold when we enter the hall; nonmembers are strictly forbidden from entering that part of the building. I'm sure you understand."

Ben nodded, he had expected as much after reading about Freemason initiations and rituals.

Mr. James continued in the lobby as he was gently tying a cloth over Ben's eyes, "Once inside I'll lead you to the center of the room and then stand by your side. You'll be asked a series of questions based on the material we covered in our weekly sessions. Don't be nervous, Ben, I sense our leadership is quite eager for you to join us. As long as you know the basics, you should be fine, son. When the questions are done, I'll lead you from the room back here to the lobby and your time here will be complete. The Brothers will deliberate and make a decision, which either the young Mr. Sullivan or I will share with you at a later time."

There was a curious pause and while the two men stood quietly, Ben wondered what was going on. "Ben, I just want to say one last thing before we go in," Mr. James finally added. "I know we've only known each other a short time, but it didn't take much time at all for me to realize what a tremendous young man you are. Ben, being a part of this organization has been one of the most rewarding experiences of my life and what we do here means everything to me. I never expressed properly how grateful I am that you're joining us. Ben, we need you, we need more men like you. If you remember one bit of advice I've ever given you it's to trust yourself," the old man said, his voice shaking far more than usual as he was overcome with emotion.

"I will, Mr. James, and I'll spend the rest of my life earning it," Ben added with a smile for his emotional old friend.

A hug took Ben by surprise, but he quickly gathered his footing and hugged his friend back. "OK, son, let's show 'em what we got!" Mr. James said as they entered the building.

Mr. James held the blindfolded Ben's arm and led him into the large meeting area. Ben could tell the room was full, but there was an open area in the center of the room where he and Mr. James were standing. There were men along each side quietly observing, not making much sound, though Ben could sense their presence.

Billy Sullivan's voice interrupted the silence from the front of the room opposite from the door the two men entered, "Mr. James, who have you brought before us and what is his purpose?"

The old man answered, "This is Benjamin Gilsum, and he seeks to petition for initiation."

"Has he been properly prepared and who has taken the responsibility to teach this man?" Billy asked.

"He has been properly prepared, Senior Deacon, and I have taught him," Mr. James replied.

Billy announced, "Very well, Mr. James, I shall question him before the full membership so we can all determine if he has properly learned from those teachings."

Mr. James released Ben's arm and took a step to the side, not leaving his young pupil alone. Ben took a deep breath and waited for Billy's questions, "Benjamin, do you come here of your own free will?"

"Yes," Ben replied.

"Benjamin, do you believe in one God?"

"Yes," Ben replied again.

"Benjamin, who is the third king and who does he represent?" Billy asked.

Enough with the Benjamin! "The third king is Melchior. He was sent with two other kings, Patisar and Caspar, to confirm the birth of Jesus Christ, God on Earth. Melchior represented all humankind."

"Very good Benjamin," Billy replied. "Now can you tell me for what purpose did man seek an agreement with God? The agreement that would eventually lead God to be born and die as a man, leaving Earth forever as man does."

Ben thought a moment and answered, "Mankind grew weary of God's wrath and sought to put an end to God's punishment on Earth for its sins."

"Ben you're doing very well," Billy said. *Ben, finally!* "Tell me Benjamin, what are the risks associated with this new-found free will that man acquired through this agreement with God?"

Ben couldn't help but slightly shake his head at being called Benjamin again. "Though humankind was given free will on Earth, with that came the risk of proving himself unworthy of the Kingdom of Heaven after death," Ben answered.

"I have only one more question for you Benjamin," Billy said, and Ben could feel Mr. James' confusion. *One more question? That's it?* "Are you willing to dedicate your life to the same mission that my Brothers here and I are committed to? Are you willing to be an example to and a leader of men by your deeds and prove to God and Lucifer alike that mankind is worthy of God's undying love and eternity in the Kingdom of Heaven?"

Ben shook off his confusion. He had expected many more questions and to be challenged, "Yes, Senior Deacon."

There was a long pause before anyone spoke and Ben could hear footsteps coming toward him followed by whispers, apparently directed at Mr. James. The familiar voice didn't belong to Billy, but Ben couldn't place it from just a whisper. Ben felt the surprise from Mr. James and then heard the footsteps going back the way they came, toward Billy's voice in the front of the room. Mr. James took Ben's arm and Billy spoke one last time before the two men left the room, "Benjamin and Mr. James, please wait in the lobby while we deliberate and Benjamin, please don't leave. My Brothers and I will discuss your petition and I will come to you with our decision. Once again, Ben, you did very well. Please leave us for a moment."

Once in the lobby, Mr. James took off Ben's blindfold. "Well, this is an unusual turn of events," Mr. James said. "But like I said, my Brothers are anxious to have you join us."

Ben could tell his old friend was both confused and concerned. The old man seemed unusually uncomfortable with the situation. "I'm ready for whatever they come out here with, Mr. James," Ben said in an attempt to calm his mentor.

"I have very little doubt of that," Mr. James replied. There was an awkward silence and Ben couldn't help but wonder why he'd spent four weeks being tutored which was actually a reduction from the original plan, for something as simple as he'd just experienced. *I could have prepared for that in five minutes!*

The men sat quietly but only for about fifteen minutes when the door to the main hall opened and Billy came through wearing a bright smile. "Congratulations, Mr. Gilsum! My Brothers and I made the easy decision to accept your petition for initiation," Billy said as he reached out and shook Ben's hand. "We've also determined that there will be no need to wait until the next Assembly. Unless either of you objects we'd like to conduct the initiation now."

Ben looked at Mr. James who was visibly confused. "I don't object," Ben said, looking to his mentor for a confirmation.

"Uh, no objection from me," Mr. James replied before he shook Ben's hand and offered an awkward congratulations.

Billy continued, "Mr. James, I realize you haven't had time to prepare Ben here for the initiation ritual, so it's been determined that we'll skip much of the formality and proceed with the quick and dirty version to save time and allow the Brothers to make their way home at a decent hour." *A decent hour? It's not even eight o'clock!*

"Very well Mr. Sullivan, let's proceed," Mr. James said to the Senior Deacon, clearly bothered by the haste and lack of protocol.

The three men entered the main hall, this time Ben without a blindfold. The room was empty in the center. There were three rows of seats on each side filled with adult men ranging from their 40s to Mr. James' age. There were five chairs lined up across a stage in the front of the room. The old building had no central air conditioning, only a wall-mounted unit at the rear of the row-house style property that helped, but it was still hot with all the people in attendance. There was an unpleasant smell in the air, mostly of an old, musty building and of too many men sweating in their suits. Ben was far more uncomfortable without his blindfold as he could feel all the eyes in the room fixed on him at once. He was feeling a bit nauseous. It appeared the room was converted from a small auditorium of some sort or playhouse. Three of the chairs on the stage were filled with other officers of the organization Ben assumed, and Billy would take the fourth. The fifth chair remained empty and Ben thought it must have belonged to Mr. James. A sixth chair was set back several feet and placed on a platform elevating it above the five chairs in front. There was someone seated in this place of honor, perhaps the leader of the group? Ben couldn't see the person's face because that entire part of the stage was dark. He could only see a shadowy figure who appeared to be presiding silently over the entire ceremony.

Once Billy took his seat, Mr. James and Ben moved to the area on the floor in front of the stage. Mr. James spoke, "Worshipful Master, I have returned with my brother, Ben Gilsum, who has completed his petition for initiation. By word of the Senior Deacon, our Brothers have approved Ben's petition and we are here to request his initiation."

The Worshipful Master, still cloaked in darkness nodded to Billy Sullivan, who then stood up and walked off the stage carrying what appeared to be a Bible over to Ben and Mr. James. Billy raised the book in both hands above his head and turned to each side of the room presenting it to the other members. He then lowered the book to chest level, placing his left hand under his right hand with his palm facing the ceiling cradling the book, showing it to Ben. Ben could see the book was not a Bible, and it appeared to be a leather-bound collection of very old texts. *The secret writings of Herrad of Landsberg!?*

Billy began, "Benjamin, we're about to conclude our activities this evening. I'm speaking for the Worshipful Master when I say congratulations on your acceptance and welcome to the Brothers of Herrad. This ceremony will be much shorter than our typical initiation per the Worshipful Master's request. Ben, we have only one requirement of you to complete your initiation and become a member of our group. If you would, Mr. Gilsum, please place your right hand on these sacred texts and answer that you agree to the following. Benjamin Gilsum, do you agree to maintain the privacy of the Brothers of Herrad by not speaking of our knowledge or customs with any non-member?"

"I do," Ben answered.

"Benjamin Gilsum, do you promise to dedicate your life to providing a positive example to your fellow man with your deeds and to donate your time and money to help those in need?"

"I do," Ben answered again.

"Finally Benjamin, do you promise to remain loyal to your Brothers present in this room and to share in their quest to be worthy of God's love?"

"I do," Ben replied with some hesitation.

"Very well, Benjamin Gilsum, on behalf of the Worshipful Master and my Brothers here this evening, I'd like to officially welcome you to the Brothers of Herrad!" Billy announced.

With that, Billy returned the sacred texts to his chair on the stage and the members in the room stood and clapped, with the exception of the Worshipful Master, who remained seated and hidden by darkness. Ben looked over at Mr. James who was smiling and clapping but still showing signs of frustration. The initiation was rushed well beyond his liking and he wasn't sure why. Ben walked with Billy around the room and was introduced to his new Brothers. Ben hadn't noticed that the Worshipful Master left his dark perch and vanished to the back of the building, taking Mr. James with him. As the other members left through the front Billy reminded Ben the group meets on the first Wednesday of each month for Assembly. He was now allowed and strongly encouraged to attend. All the men left and Ben made his way back to his car. The evening concluded as oddly as it had begun and Ben drove home wondering why it was all so rushed. *Where the hell did Mr. James disappear to?*

Chapter 32

Ben and Ted spent the morning talking about baseball and little else. This morning chat was an almost weekly ritual for the first year and a half of Ben's tenure at the company, but in recent weeks Ben had been avoiding his superior. Ben was visibly nervous when Ted walked into the office kitchen behind him to join the younger man in making himself a cup of coffee. Ben's recent moment alone with Ted had done little to change his uneasiness; however, their conversation helped Ben to feel more comfortable around his boss. The several unauthorized searches seemed to be unnoticed or at least unquestioned, which also helped Ben to feel more at ease.

After his conversation with Ted, Ben returned to his office with nothing to do but stare at a blank screen wondering if he dared dig further into the communications he had discovered between Billy and Bradford Sullivan. He talked himself into doing it by rationalizing that no one realized Ben knew Bradford Sullivan was Mr. White. It was likely no one else at the company knew Bradford Sullivan was Mr. White, either. If his searches into Billy Sullivan didn't raise suspicion why not expect the same should he search Bradford Sullivan?

It didn't take long to find the evidence Ben knew was there. Bradford Sullivan was helping Billy Sullivan keep attention away from his clients' transgressions. The father and son discussed it brazenly as if no one would ever try to investigate their activities. Maybe no one would and Ben wasn't about to bring his findings to Ted and face the consequences of his own illegal actions. Ben kept searching and reading and eventually discovered something disturbing about the activities of Bradford Sullivan. Bradford also operated under a private business name functioning as a political consultant; there were countless communications with elected officials that were eerily similar to those between Billy and his clients. Most of the communications were about social engagements followed by a consultant fee and very large charitable contributions to an undisclosed organization. These donations appeared to be in exchange for secrecy about certain activities that could cause potential embarrassment for the client. The donation amounts were staggering and so were the fees. *That's a whole lot of pancake breakfasts!*

Ben stopped his search when he discovered communications between Bradford Sullivan and the junior senator from the state of Massachusetts. *Holy shit! That's Angel's boss!*

Chapter 33

Watching baseball at a sports bar or a ballpark was far more enjoyable than watching it home alone, but around DC that almost always meant watching the Washington Nationals or the Baltimore Orioles. Though the Nationals and Orioles were fine teams, sitting and watching them for three hours would not give an avid St. Louis Cardinals fan what they wanted, unless of course, they were playing the Cardinals. On most nights during baseball season, Ben would live-stream FOX Sports Midwest on Sling TV and watch his beloved Cardinals play. Just as Ben was settling in he heard the familiar sound of light knocking at his door. He knew it was Mr. James before he got up. *Doesn't this guy have a phone?*

"I hope I'm not disturbing you," Mr. James said, wearing his wool trousers with sneakers and a sweater, as Ben invited him in.

"Not at all, I'm happy to see you. I was concerned the other night. I didn't get a chance to say thank you or goodbye," Ben answered.

"To be honest Ben, I was unnerved at your initiation and upon its conclusion, I went straight to the Worshipful Master to discuss the manner in which it was conducted. It was completely unusual and though I knew it was being accelerated, I had no idea we would do your initiation on the same night as your petition. We skipped quite a bit of ceremony, which is fine, but there is some further training that takes place at an initiation that I wanted to be sure you received before our first Assembly. I took up my concerns with the Worshipful Master and asked for his permission to complete the training with you. I'm here tonight to discuss that with you and ask when may be a good time for you."

Ben gave his mentor a confused look, "Mr. James, you didn't have to drive all the way out here for that. Why didn't you just call me?" he asked.

"Well, you know I don't like talking on the phone much at all, son. I'd rather talk in person," the old man said with a smile.

Ben thought for a moment, "You know I'm not doing anything right now, I realize it's getting late, but since you drove here would you like to do the training tonight?"

Mr. James looked at his Patek Philippe, Rose Gold Automatic wristwatch, and paused, "I think we can accomplish what we need to this evening. Could I trouble you for a glass of water?"

Mr. James took his usual seat at Ben's small dining table and sipped his water before speaking, "Ben, I'm sure you remember our conversation about the three kings."

Ben nodded.

"Well son, we were supposed to go into further detail and ceremony of what those kings each symbolize now that humankind has taken control of its own activities on Earth. They have a purpose that the Brothers of Herrad believe continues on to this day. In fact, while the teachings of Herrad were still part of Freemason belief, especially during the forming of the United States, you could see how those principles apply to our government."

Ben perked up at this suggestion. *Well, this should certainly be interesting!*

"Remember, the First King was a witness for God, and today the First King symbolizes truth and justice. The Brothers believe a person or organization that is ruled first by truth would be a follower of the First King. The Second King was a witness for Satan, and today the Second

King symbolizes power and perhaps more specifically, power and wealth. The Brothers believe a person or organization ruled first by this type of power would be a follower of the Second King. Finally, the Third King was a witness for humankind and today the Third King symbolizes the health and well-being of the individual. The Brothers believe a person or organization ruled by compassion and respect for their fellow human first would be a follower of the Third King." Mr. James added, "A person ruled by the Third King would likely be empathetic toward those around them as would an organization."

Ben interrupted, "But how can you see this ideology in our government today?" Ben was far more interested in the answer to this question than the rest of the teachings Mr. James was sharing.

The old man took another sip of his water before he began to speak again. Ben could feel the excitement and enthusiasm coming from his mentor. Mr. James didn't get to discuss this very much anymore, and it thrilled him to have such a worthy and eager pupil. "Well, it's related to one of the first things young civics students learn in grade school, Ben. It's as simple as the three branches of government. The Judicial Branch represents justice, truth, and fairness of laws. The Executive Branch is about power and influence. The Legislative Branch is in place to make certain individuals maintain a level of involvement and power. The Brothers and the Freemasons believed any organization should be balanced this way and that there should never be too much influence in any one of the three philosophies. While many would think those ruled by the Second King would be corrupt and somehow evil, the influence they provide is necessary as is the influence of the other two kings. Balance is the most important function of any organization, small or large."

Mr. James could see that Ben was considering everything he had heard, and he had made an impression on the young man, "Ben, that's the heart of the discussion we missed at your initiation. It was extremely important that you receive this information prior to your membership so you could have a full understanding of our basic principles. Do you have questions about this or anything we've discussed?"

Ben had a question, but he wasn't sure how to ask or if he should. He suspected the answer but he wanted the old man to tell him without being asked, "Mr. James, when did the legendary split from the Freemasons take place?" Ben decided to just get right to the point, "I feel like this wasn't hundreds of years ago during the formation of our country."

Mr. James was always impressed by Ben's intuition, "Ben, you have such an amazing mind. I'll tell you the full story another time but for now, let's say some fifty years ago a young banker who was a proud Freemason saw the 'writing on the wall' if you will. In his mind, money and power had begun to rule the organization. Justice and humanity had not disappeared and they're still very much a part of the group today, but the balance simply wasn't there. This young banker who had a great deal of influence tried to bring balance back and was met with a great deal of resistance. You know the rest of the story son and now you understand why and when. Amazing, young man."

The younger man shrugged off the compliment as he did with most compliments. *Why won't he just come out and admit he was the young banker who started the Brothers of Herrad? Is he really that humble or just playing me?*

"I understand it's getting late, but I have one more question," Ben added. "You said that successful organizations are ruled by a balance of influence from the three kings. Are there people within the Brothers that show themselves to be ruled by any specific king?"

Mr. James' eyes grew wide. This was a complicated question, and he wasn't about to give a direct answer.

Ben immediately felt he made a mistake asking his mentor such a direct question about his fellow Brothers.

"Well, son, it's certainly fair to ask but I think you'll have to find the answer to that question on your own. We have members of our leadership who show traits you may recognize in tonight's lesson." *Yes, I'd say money and power certainly influence at least one!*

133

Mr. James continued, "I will say while I believe we have a strong representation of those influenced by the first two kings in our leadership, I'm very excited about finding a member who is clearly influenced by the Third King, young Ben Gilsum." Mr. James leaned closer to his pupil, "And those are the hardest to find."

Chapter 34

Sitting at his desk at work, Ben was busy reflecting on his current status with the secret society known as the Brothers of Herrad. With his training and initiation complete, Ben was an official member and it happened so quickly that it gave him little time to think about whether he wanted to be a member. In recent months, Ben had taken on this new and adventurous identity and perhaps this was the way things would be for a while. Ben thought about all the warning signs he had seen in the weeks leading up to his initiation, including the criminal activity he discovered by the Senior Deacon and his father. He thought about ending his association with the Brothers on several occasions. But each time Ben was sure he would drop out of consideration he thought about Mr. James. Ben thought about how talking with him seemed to help him better understand himself and make improvements that would benefit him for the rest of his life. He also considered how happy Angelina was about his involvement with the organization and the excitement she showed when they talked about what Ben was doing.

Ben struggled with the knowledge of how the organization he was now a part of was being funded. He knew some of the good deeds the Brothers were doing and would learn a great deal more about the many charitable acts, but was that enough to overlook the crimes that were taking place? Were there more crimes he was unaware of? Ben would repeat those two questions to himself until he could come up with an acceptable answer and he had no idea how long that would take. *Like it or not I'm one of them now. And I swore loyalty!*

With a sigh, Ben got back to work. Being busy helped take his mind off his moral dilemma, but Ben's efficiency at work once again left him with a great deal of free time from early afternoon to the end of his workday. Based on where his unauthorized searches left him last, with his girlfriend's boss coming into the intricate web of illegal activity, there was no chance he would stop now. Ben continued looking into the communications and activity of Bradford Sullivan and the junior senator of Massachusetts. The young intelligence analyst failed to realize that this unauthorized search would bring him to a place that would show an obvious abuse of company, and much more dangerously, abuse of government resources. While searching Bradford Sullivan, Ben came across communications with the young and beautiful Angelina Rindge. Before Ben came to his senses and realized he was reading up on his own girlfriend, he read several communications between her and Bradford Sullivan that made him leave his office and head to the men's room where he could no longer hold down the chicken salad sandwich he had packed for lunch that morning.

There were emails exchanged between Bradford and Angelina that were sent before Ben met her. Bradford told Angelina about the places she could meet Ben, what he was like, his hobbies, his background and instructed her to make contact with him and develop a relationship with the young man. Bradford was specific about how far the relationship should go and what Angelina's objectives were. Angelina was told to always encourage community involvement and charitable activity. She was told the Freemasons would be an excellent topic of discussion and to use the known organization to lead to the Brothers of Herrad in conversation whenever possible. Bradford instructed her that any activity that involved helping children should be pursued. Her main objective was to keep the young man happy as long as she could and eventually she could cut ties completely and either move back to Boston or stay and continue her work in DC using whatever she saw fit as an excuse to end the relationship. She was told to be aggressive in the beginning because Ben was a terrible introvert. She would have to make all the first moves and not give up if he seemed disinterested. The final communication Ben read before becoming ill involved payment the young woman was to receive. Angelina Rindge had done her job, and she had done it remarkably well.

Chapter 35

Discovering the truth about Angelina made Ben physically ill and unable to focus. He needed to get away. He needed to think. Ben went to Ted's office and told his boss he wasn't feeling well and would need to go home for the day. He went home and turned his cell phone off, skipping his Thursday night ritual at the Firehouse. Angelina was there but she would dine alone that night with only occasional yet cheerful encounters with Patty. Both young women were curious about where Ben was, but neither of them brought up the topic, at least with each other.

The unauthorized searches that day at work would be the last of Ben's unlawful indiscretions. He had seen far more than he wanted to about the web he found himself entangled in and the connections between people he had no idea even knew each other. Ted warned the young man to be careful and, like a fool, he walked straight into this entanglement with his eyes shut in a dreamlike state. Ben slept through the night and continued to sleep through his alarm the next morning, taking a sick day from work. Typically, when something weighed heavily on the young man he was up all night thinking about what he was going to do about it and planning his actions. But when completely overwhelmed, which was rare, Ben would shut down and sleep came easily. The early riser slept until noon and remained awake in bed staring at the ceiling for a couple hours after. With this wake-up came clarity and once Ben gathered himself he knew exactly what to do.

Once his plan was set, Ben refused to sit around the house any longer moping and feeling sorry for himself, although he still wanted to be alone. He needed a ride in the Jeep. A long ride to clear his mind and think. Shame and heartbreak were quickly giving way to anger and sharp focus. *How could I have been so stupid!* Ben needed to get away and calm his ire so he made a few phone calls and booked a room for himself in Rehoboth Beach, Delaware, for the next two nights. He turned off his cell phone, packed a very light bag, and drove three hours east to The Avenue Inn and Spa. Ben had never been to Rehoboth and was planning on inviting Angelina there for a weekend getaway after a coworker had described the area to him. "If you like the beach, it's the perfect spot. There's an awesome boardwalk, lots of restaurants, shops and action everywhere with plenty of seafood and bars. Take your girlfriend and stay at The Avenue if you wanna impress her. It's gorgeous!" *That'll do nicely.*

Chapter 36

Monday morning Ben returned to work with one goal in mind. He was going to confess everything to Ted about his unauthorized searches and accept whatever punishment would come. Ben was acutely aware that he would be subject to criminal charges and terminated immediately from his position at the company. This was a risky proposition for Ben, but he knew it was only a matter of time before he would have to face the consequences of his actions and it would likely be better for him if he confessed rather than waiting for someone to discover what he had done. It was also the first step Ben felt he had to take to get his life back on track. He had avoided contact with Angelina all weekend; his plan was to discuss things with her later if he wasn't incarcerated. His first Assembly as a member of the Brothers was the same week, which was another matter he would need to attend to.

Ben started his day as he always did, attacking whatever tasks were due and catching up on all of his work immediately and efficiently. Old habits die hard. *They're going to throw me in jail and I'm worried about not getting my work done?* Ben was up to date on all of his assignments before lunch. He took a deep breath, lifted his feet off the ground, and pushed on the edge of his desk with both hands rolling away in his chair so he could get up and go talk to Ted. *Here goes nothing!*

"Come on in, young fella. Close the door," Ted said as he noticed his subordinate standing in the doorway of his office. Ben couldn't hide the fear he was feeling as he shut the door and slowly took a seat in the "therapy chair."

"Ted, there's something I really need to talk to you about," he managed to say in a nervous voice.

"Before you get into that son, there are some things I want to tell you." *He already knows.* Ted knew Ben was hurting. He knew why and he wasn't about to let him fall on this sword, "Ben, I know you've been going off script for a few weeks. I also knew at some point you would come into my office telling me all about it and worried that I would have you fired and taken out of here in handcuffs."

The fear Ben was feeling quickly turned to absolute horror. *How could I have been so careless!?* Ted's tone changed to that of a concerned parent speaking to a child who had done something wrong but was clearly sorry about it, "Son, when you started reading into your girlfriend you nearly got yourself into a mess I couldn't get you out of. That was reckless and I don't think you need me to explain why." *Wait. Get me out of?*

"Ben, it's very important that you stop what you're doing immediately, do you understand?"

Ben couldn't speak and only offered an affirming nod to his boss as he was looking down at the desk that separated the two men.

"Ben. Son, look at me. You're done going off script, is that correct?" Ted said, needing more than a nod.

"Yes, I'm done. I found more than I ever imagined I'd find. I'm done, I don't even want to know more," Ben replied.

Ted waited a short time before he spoke again. He waited for Ben to stop fidgeting and looking away. When Ben looked up again in anticipation, Ted spoke. His tone had changed again. He was no longer the caring parent. This time he was nervous and ashamed.

"Ben, you don't need to worry about any of this. This conversation will never leave this room," Ted said without waiting for an affirmation from Ben. "There's more to this story and I'm about to share some very sensitive information with you that may change your current course of action, but you'll have to decide all of that for yourself, young man."

Ben was only slightly relieved and intrigued to hear what his boss was about to say.

Ted continued, "I knew about most of what you discovered on your own. Nothing about your girlfriend, I promise you that, but I've been aware of what was going on with William and Bradford for some time now. The thing with Angelina unfortunately doesn't surprise me, her father is close with one of Bradford's clients and they're all from Boston and circulate with all the same people." *Jesus, I never considered any of that.*

"Son, these things start so simply. I knew White was up to something the day I met him, which was a long time before you did and I know you felt the same way about him when you met him."

Ben nodded in agreement.

"Well, I did my own investigation and when it became clear to Bradford that I knew what he was up to he surprised me. He confessed everything and explained it away as being the norm in town and that none of the people he was working with were bad and he was protecting them from pointless political scandal. No one was being hurt, and he was raising thousands of dollars for a local charity. By the time I realized he wasn't completely honest with me and that his son was up to something in the private sector it was too late for me to take proper action. I'd followed him too far and would be taken down just as hard as he and William would. So I was weak, unlike you. I shielded them in order to protect myself. I'm not proud of what I've done and I'll be damned if I'm going to sit here and let you take responsibility for something I should have handled years ago!"

Ben remained speechless but his worry had shifted and he was now concerned for his friend.

"So, Ben. What do we do next? I'm sure that question has found its way into that brilliant head of yours and if you had the words, you'd have asked it by now. You are clean and clear and I'm going to make absolutely certain of that. You need do nothing further, young man, I will handle this one. You have some personal things to be concerned about and that's all. Thank goodness for me, I don't need to be involved in any of that!" Ted managed a half-hearted smile, "You will leave this office with your head held high, Ben. You did everything right and I'm proud of you. The company is proud of you and our superiors at the government will be proud of you. I want you to be assured of that as things play out and think about that before you make any rash decisions."

Finally finding his voice, Ben spoke, "Ted, you're a good man. You didn't know the full story. Mr. White tricked you!" *That manipulative bastard!*

There was no response from Ted and he clearly said all he was going to say on the matter. Ben reached out his hand to his boss and friend who took it and gave it a hearty shake. The two stared at each other, neither offering any more words but knowing the love and respect they felt for one another was mutual. Ben left Ted's office wondering if he would ever see him again.

Chapter 37

I t was the first Wednesday of the month and Ben was early again, sitting in his Jeep outside the Brothers of Herrad lodge. He was dressed in his only suit, the same one he wore at his initiation. This would be his first Assembly as an actual member of the group and no one had told him exactly what he was supposed to do other than show up at seven o'clock on the first Wednesday of the month. So, at six-thirty he waited for a familiar face that he might tag along with into the building. There was activity inside the building already, but judging by the lack of cars parked outside Ben assumed most of the members hadn't arrived yet.

The first familiar face Ben saw belonged to Billy Sullivan, who caught Ben's attention in his rear-view mirror as he walked up to Ben's car waving his hand and smiling. "There's my newest Brother! Eager to get started, Brother Gilsum?" Billy said as Ben got out of his car.

Ben tried not to show his disappointment as he returned the smile and shook the young man's hand. "Let's do this, Brother," Ben said while looking around the street for Mr. James, hoping he would be there too.

"You have no idea how excited I am to have you with us. I mean look around when you get in there. Yours and mine are the only heads not covered with gray hair my friend," Billy joked.

"Or no hair," Ben returned.

"True," Billy laughed. "Let me walk you in Ben. You can take any seat on the side you want. As you know the front of the room is reserved for officers. Just so you know, Mr. Gilsum, I will be pushing you to join us up there as quickly as possible. We need some fresh blood running this place, buddy. I'm not the only one who feels that way either, and we all believe the attention given to you by the old man means he's got big plans for you. We're all pretty excited." *The old man? Mr. James?*

Ben managed to find a seat near the back of the room and a couple rows back, trying to keep himself unnoticeable. There was nowhere in the assembly hall Ben could sit and accomplish that endeavor. He was a shiny new penny in a basket full of old and worn out coins. Every member approached him and welcomed him and asked him all the same questions over and over. Attention from strangers followed by small talk was something that made Ben feel terribly uncomfortable, especially without someone he knew to bail him out when he struggled to find his words. Ben did his best to hide his agony, but he was failing terribly. *Get me the hell out of here!*

"There's my star pupil," Mr. James said, walking over in his always fashionable wool trousers with sneakers and a sweater, to say hello to Ben. He could see Ben's discomfort and quickly shooed everyone away from the young man. "My Brothers, please! Let's not send our newest member running away on his first day. Leave the man alone. Tonight's an easy night for you, Mr. Gilsum. Just relax and take in the show. There's plenty for you to do later my son," Mr. James said, putting his hand on Ben's shoulder and giving him a wink.

"Hello Mr. James," was all a visibly grateful Ben could manage as the old man headed toward the stage to take his seat at the front of the room.

Feeling more relaxed, Ben scanned the room studying all the older men's faces. He had seen most of them the last time he was there with a few exceptions. He turned his gaze to the front of the room and noticed all the same officers in the five chairs. Ben also noticed the sixth chair elevated behind the five was not in darkness as it had been during his initiation. The chair was empty, but he could see it clearly. *Well, this should be interesting.* At exactly seven o'clock, all the men in the room took a seat and quieted. Billy stood after a few moments and addressed the room. "My Brothers, welcome," Billy said loudly.

"Good evening, Senior Deacon," all the men returned.

"Please rise and welcome our Worshipful Master," Billy continued. Everyone stood as the Worshipful Master came into the room from the back of the stage and took his seat, staring directly at Ben as he sat down. *You have got to be kidding me!*

Ben stared back in horror at the smiling face of Bradford Sullivan, or the man officially known to Ben as Mr. White. *I should have known.* Ben remained frozen as everyone else in the room sat down. Mr. White leaned toward Ben and laughed, "Brother Gilsum? Please, young man, you're embarrassing me. Do take your seat, sir." The rest of the Brothers laughed as Ben woke from his painful astonishment and slowly sat down.

The newest member remained stoic for the rest of the Assembly. There was a brief official welcome for Ben that he was requested to stand again and be recognized. What followed were summaries of charitable efforts in progress and other efforts planned by specific members with presentations, some budget discussions with new purchases and expenses, and several other topics that Ben wasn't paying any attention to. The room had become quiet and Ben escaped from his thoughts long enough to realize the Assembly was coming to an end. Billy stood again to address the room, "My Brothers, if none of you wish to introduce a new order of business this evening, our Assembly is concluded."

There was silence from the room. Mr. White got up from his chair and the members stood while he exited again through the back of the stage. Ben didn't stand and remained frozen in his seat as the rest of the Brothers left their chairs and mingled around the center of the room. *I can't believe it.*

Several of the Brothers had left and as the room emptied, Mr. James, Billy, and Mr. White made their way over to Ben, who hadn't moved from his seat.

Billy spoke first, "Ben, it's with great pleasure that I introduce you to our Worshipful Master, leader of the Brothers and of course my dad. Ben Gilsum, this is Bradford Sullivan."

The visibly stunned Ben shook Bradford's hand but couldn't look the Worshipful Master in the eyes for more than a second. He focused his gaze downward at the familiar gold ring Bradford wore, with the letter M on the bezel. It was the same ring Ben often stared at when the older man spoke to him at work. Ben pretended to be surprised to hear Mr. White's actual name spoken out loud for the first time. He was surprised that it was given so freely, but this was a social event.

Bradford Sullivan seemed pleased by his son's introduction. "Ben Gilsum," he said, "I knew you and I would work together at some point!"

Chapter 38

Ben texted Angelina before leaving work on Thursday, his first communication with her since discovering their relationship was forged upon a paid agreement with a third party to "keep him happy." He told her he would be at the Firehouse later, he really needed to talk to her and he'd hoped she would be there. Angelina didn't text back, and she knew what "we really need to talk" meant. After so many ignored phone calls and texts, she absolutely planned to be there.

The recently enlightened Ben Gilsum arrived first and sat at a high-top table away from anyone else in the bar area. He had no interest in talking to anyone, which until recent months would be considered completely normal behavior for the young man. That didn't discourage an eager Patty from immediately coming over to say hello, excited to see Ben, "Well hello, Mr. Gilsum, fancy seeing you here, sir. You know you stood up two pretty ladies last Thursday who were dying to see you? Very disappointing no-show, my friend!"

Patty immediately sensed there was something wrong with Ben, who barely looked at her and gave a short, cold reply, "Yeah, sorry about that. I wasn't feeling great last week."

Patty's tone changed quickly to concern for her friend and she stood there silent, waiting for him to look at her before speaking. "Ben, whatever's bothering you is none of my business and I'll leave you alone but I want to be sure you know that I'm here for you. I'll always be here for you and not just here at this bar, but anywhere you want to go and talk."

Ben could feel the sincerity in Patty's words and they warmed the young man's demeanor for just a moment, "Patty, thank you. Everything is crazy right now and I have some things I need to take care of, but I'd like that. I'm gonna hold you to it." Ben managed to say just enough to make Patty smile before returning to his lonely, brooding temperament. Patty left him there alone, encouraged by what he said.

The excited hellos and laughter coming from the other end of the building told Ben that Angelina had arrived, and he took a deep breath and stopped rehearsing the words he had planned for her. Ben stood as she came over to join him, turning away from a kiss hello.

Angelina's beautiful and contagious smile immediately left her face. "Ben, what the hell is wrong?" she asked, looking as if she were about to cry.

"Can we go outside to talk?" Ben replied.

The regulars and staff who had become accustomed to enjoying the energy from the attractive young couple saw the two walking out together wearing faces they had not seen before when the couple was together.

"Why have you been ignoring me?" Angelina said, speaking first when they got outside.

"Angel, it's over. All of it. It's over! You can stop pretending to give a shit about me!"

Ben stopped for a moment when he saw a tear falling down Angelina's cheek. *What the hell is that?*

"I know you were paid to be my girlfriend! I can't believe I fell for it! You did your job, Angel, you did a damn good job, but now it's over. You can stop looking at me like anything I say matters to you. You can go back to your boss, who's a fucking criminal by the way, and you can go back to the Sullivans and tell them whatever you want. I'm done with all of you!"

Angelina was sobbing when Ben was done talking.

"What the hell are you even doing?" Ben asked. "I know it's all bullshit, Angel!"

Angelina got control of herself and tried to speak, "Ben, I'm so sorry. I don't know what else to say."

Ben interrupted, "Say nothing! Walk away from me. Go back to your dirty politicians and phony upstanding citizens, pretending to do great things for the world as they lie right to your face and pull you into their twisted world full of bullshit! Look at me! I'm done with all of it, Angel. I'm done with you!" Ben turned away and walked to his Jeep, not looking back.

Angelina stood alone, crying on the sidewalk outside the Columbia Firehouse, stunned. She watched Ben walk to his Jeep, get in, and drive away. She was heartbroken. Her feelings for Ben had long grown far beyond the excitement of an assignment from government contacts and the promise of advancement from her boss. She had fallen in love with the shy, young man from Arkansas.

Angelina Rindge gathered herself, wiped away her tears and spoke aloud to no one in particular, "I love you, Benjamin Gilsum. Goodbye."

Chapter 39

There were no regrets about breaking up with Angelina. Ben knew there was no way he could trust anything she had to say for herself if she'd tried to stop him. Thankfully, she didn't. But the tears? They were genuine. She was hurting, and he wasn't prepared for that reaction, yet he knew he did the right thing. Ben couldn't erase the image from his mind of the girl he had fallen for staring at him, crying. He had thought it would be easy to end his relationship with her after discovering it was based on lies, but it wasn't. He was heartbroken and needed someone to talk to. There was only one person who would make him feel better without asking any questions about why or who did what, especially once she realized he needed her.

"Baby, two days in a row? You know it's Thursday right, and we talked yesterday? Oh, what am I saying Ben, it's lovely to hear from my son no matter what day of the week it is. How you doing up there, baby?" an excited Mrs. Gilsum said as she picked up the phone, after two rings.

It only took one brief pause from Ben for Mrs. Gilsum to know something was wrong with her only son, "Ben, what's on your mind? Tell me everything. Momma's here, baby."

Ben let out a sigh, "Mom, me and Angel broke up."

Mrs. Gilsum had heard enough, "Oh, honey, I'm so sorry. Maybe you should call her or go see her. You know sometimes these things work themselves out. Just give her some time," Mrs. Gilsum contradicted herself.

"No. Not this time Mom, this one isn't going to work out," Ben replied, hoping his mother wouldn't ask what happened.

Mrs. Gilsum thankfully did not disappoint. She knew her son was like her husband, and didn't like to talk about it when something was hurting him. She knew he wanted comforting but not too much. She knew he wanted support but few questions and little coddling. She knew exactly what he wanted to hear and she was the only person who could say it for him the way he needed.

"Ben, you know your mother loves you. You're a good, strong man and you'll get through this, it's just gonna take time. We've all had our hearts broken, son. One thing I will say, baby, and you take this to heart, you may not see it now and you're not going to until the hurt stops. But Ben, she changed you and for the better. You're a different man than you were a few months ago and I hope you hold on to that. Baby, you're a better person for knowing her and I'm always gonna love her for that."

If she only knew the whole story!

"Time will take care of your heart Ben, take something positive away from all of this. Don't you waste any more time than you need to on the hurt. Don't dwell on the negative, baby."

The call was short, but it didn't end until Ben promised his mother three times he would not dwell on the hurt for too long and he would call her anytime he felt he needed to talk. Ben wanted to tell her more and there was much more to tell but he decided it would be best for his parents if he kept the update to just one piece of difficult news at a time. He wasn't sure how to tell the rest anyway, and, as he was hoping, his mother made him feel better. Though he felt a little better Ben was feeling more homesick than he ever had since leaving Decatur two years earlier. He didn't miss being in Decatur and he hadn't since he left but he missed his mother dearly, especially now. He wanted to call her every moment since he discovered Angelina's deception and more so after the breakup but he knew it would only make her worry.

The young man from Arkansas was just starting to feel comfortable in DC, like he found a place he actually belonged after spending his entire life feeling like a square peg who didn't quite fit anywhere. Now his confidence was dashed, his heart was broken, and he didn't believe there was anyone around him he could trust. He was hurting and feeling a long, long way from home.

Chapter 40

en went to work Friday feeling the same apprehension he'd been experiencing for weeks. *Will I make it through the day?* Though he felt a heavy weight was lifted from his conscience after speaking with Ted, he was still nervous about the imminent fallout that would result from when Ted "handled this one." He was comforted by his boss' promise to keep him out of trouble but how much power did Ted have to protect him? Ben broke company policy, and he also broke the law. He would make good on his promise to never do it again but would that be enough? What the hell was he going to do when he saw Mr. White again?

Thankfully, Ben didn't see Mr. White at the office and it was Friday so he'd have at least two more days to think about how he would react before he saw him again.

A coworker popped into Ben's office asking if he knew where Ted was today.

"I don't know, is he not here?" Ben asked.

"No, he's not going to be in today apparently," his coworker replied.

"Maybe he's sick," Ben suggested.

The coworker answered, "That's the first time in the ten years I've been here that Ted Seneca called in sick. I was just wondering if you knew something. No one else does."

Chapter 41

Before leaving his first Assembly as a member of the Brothers of Herrad, Ben had spoken briefly with Mr. James and told him there was something he needed to discuss with him in private. Ben offered to buy his old friend a drink or even dinner in thanks for all the time he spent working with him. "Time well spent, my son. Time very well spent," Mr. James was flattered at the invitation but told Ben he would prefer to stop by Saturday morning and pay him a visit at home. He didn't like to leave his house after dark and taking a morning drive to visit a friend was just enough activity to keep an old man like him happy. Mr. James could tell there was something troubling his young pupil, and he didn't want to wait too long to speak with him about it.

On Saturday morning Ben was up early and ready for his visitor, anxious to talk. He'd been up all night trying to figure out how to deliver the delicate information he had regarding the Worshipful Master and his son, the Senior Deacon. Ben confessing to Ted meant risking his career and being incarcerated. Ending his relationship with his beautiful girlfriend with whom he had fallen in love was difficult, though he had no choice given the circumstances. But somehow this conversation with Mr. James gave him far more stress. If it weren't for the bond they had formed this would be as simple as telling the old man he was moving on and thanking him for his time and consideration but membership with the Brothers of Herrad just wasn't for him. But it wasn't going to be that simple. Ben had grown to love and respect his mentor. He knew this organization meant everything to Mr. James. His dear friend started an organization that despite the lack of morality from its current leadership, was doing incredible work for the community and particularly the children in that community. Ben wasn't sure if Mr. James had the authority anymore to remove the Sullivans from the Brothers. He was hoping he did, or perhaps that he and the other members could remove them with some type of hearing and vote if they were made aware of the truth. Ben knew he had to share what he had uncovered, and if there was no action taken he knew what he would have to do next.

It was hot outside and Ben was waiting on his front porch when Mr. James arrived, complete with wool pants, sneakers, and a sweater. Ben greeted his friend and couldn't help but finally ask, "Mr. James, don't you ever get hot in that outfit?"

Mr. James laughed at his young friend, "Ben, son, at my age I don't think it's possible to get hot in any outfit!"

The two went inside to their typical spot at Ben's tiny dining-room table where Ben had a glass of water waiting for his mentor. Mr. James took a seat and a drink before getting straight to business, "Ben, there's something troubling you? Please, speak openly with me and tell me whatever it is."

Ben struggled at first to get to the point but decided to be direct with his old friend, "Mr. James, I can't tell you exactly how I came across the information I'm about to share with you. All I can tell you is that it's absolutely true and what happens next is completely beyond my control. I can't share any more information than what I'm about to tell you, which is more than I should be sharing."

Mr. James looked a bit stunned, but had no doubt what his friend was about to tell him would be the truth, "Ben I'm aware of your profession and the sensitive nature of the material you come in contact with. If telling me something puts you at risk I have to ask you to stop. I'm sure you've handled everything properly and there's not much an old man like me could do beyond that."

Ben paused, wondering how his mentor knew of his profession but didn't have to think very hard to figure it out. It made him hesitate to go any further. *Is the old man in cahoots with those dirty bastards and just better at covering his tracks?*

"I'm not sure we should continue this conversation," Mr. James said. "I can't be part of anything that might get you into trouble son. I simply won't put you at risk."

Ben thought for a moment and decided he had to trust himself, something his mentor had told him to do many times. Ben took a deep breath and stared into the eyes of his friend, who he sensed was more worried about Ben than himself. He knew the great risk he was taking should his mentor be part of the Sullivans' scheme; it would unravel any safety net Ted had put into place for him, but he trusted his friend.

Before Mr. James spoke again, Ben nearly shouted, "The Sullivans are involved in highly illegal activity involving elected officials and leaders of corporations!"

There was a long silence and the two men sat looking at each other. Ben was the first to speak, elaborating on what he had said before, "They've both been using phony consulting companies to work with powerful people, but instead of advice on how to run their company or campaign, they use Bradford's influence to keep certain misdeeds hidden from the authorities. They offer this in exchange for large cash donations to the Brothers of Herrad and an even greater cut for themselves."

Ben was about to speak again to apologize to his friend for what he knew would be troubling news, but Mr. James interrupted the younger man, "Ben, I have no doubt what you're telling me is true. And I understand the tremendous risk you've taken by sharing this with me. You took a great leap of faith son, a great leap indeed."

Ben was questioning if he made the right decision as his mentor paused and took a sip of water before continuing. "I had my suspicions of those two. I had doubts. I knew I needed help to determine if they were genuine."

The old man paused again, carefully considering his words knowing his prize pupil was in agony waiting to be assured he made the right decision, "I knew you were special Ben, but I had no idea how quickly you would provide the leadership and courage our organization needed to move toward the proper path once again."

There was another pause and the old man's expression changed to show warm appreciation for his young pupil. Ben immediately felt more relaxed and knew he made the right choice.

"There have been only two leaders of the Brothers of Herrad. I assumed the role of Worshipful Master at its inception when I was a younger man and eventually handed that responsibility over to Bradford Sullivan. I knew his ambition would accelerate expansion and provide the funding needed to grow the organization to the size and effectiveness I had originally hoped for. I can assure you I had no idea there would be any illegal activity associated with that funding. Our group was founded on the principle that humankind is worthy of the Kingdom of Heaven, and our vows have always included respect and compliance with the laws of the nation we operate in." Mr. James stopped speaking and studied his young friend's face for a moment and changed the course of the conversation.

"I promise you the details of what you've shared with me and how I came to know what you've told me will not be spoken to anyone outside this room. We both have a great deal of considering to do on what our next move will be. I can assure you when I'm done there will be no more of this behavior from any member of the Brothers of Herrad, no matter how powerful they believe they've become. I will remove this cancer immediately. We need funding to complete our mission, but we don't need a single penny gained by the exact type of immorality we stand opposed to."

It was the first time Ben had ever seem Mr. James show any signs of anger or aggression. Ben knew Mr. James was a highly moral man who valued integrity, but he had no idea of the fire that remained inside the old man.

Mr. James continued, "As for you, Ben. I know what you must be thinking and feeling. I know you have a decision to make, and if I'm not too late, I'd like to ask you to consider staying with us. Please use the time until our next assembly to determine what you want to do. We're not properly represented by Bradford and Billy Sullivan. If you'll allow us the time, we'll prove it to you."

Mr. James stood and indicated it was time for him to go, and without a word, Ben walked his mentor out the door and to his car. Mr. James shook the young man's hand and repeated something he had told him before, "Ben you're an amazing young man." This time he added, "I believe I'll see you again Ben Gilsum, and the moment will be much happier, son." Mr. James got in his car and drove away.

I'm not sure what to believe anymore.

Chapter 42

Angelina Rindge sat alone at Killer ESP, a coffee shop in Old Town just a few blocks away from the Columbia Firehouse. There were many styles of chairs all around the place, which immediately caught any newcomer's attention. The exposed brick walls, local art, and "funky setting with funky chairs" made it a favorite spot for Angelina. She often came to this local spot to enjoy a cup of gourmet coffee and perhaps even a homemade pastry on weekend mornings, but today she did not appear to be enjoying herself. Angelina's eyes were puffy and red and she looked as if she hadn't slept, showered, or changed clothes in a few days. The staff behind the counter typically loved her company, but they had never seen her in this condition before. No one had the courage to ask the always beautiful and cheerful young woman what was wrong. She gave the impression she wanted to be left alone, so they thought it best to do just that.

Angelina wasn't alone for long. A sharply dressed young man approached and sat across from her at the small two-person table. Billy Sullivan looked like a confident, corporate executive on his way to a board meeting. His dark hair was slicked back, corporate big-shot style, and he was wearing a ridiculously expensive suit making him stand out in a room that was currently filled with sandals, torn jeans, and t-shirts.

"Nice spot, Angel, do they throw in a tetanus shot with every cup?" Billy smiled as he sat down, but quickly changed his tone as he studied Angelina more closely, "Jesus, you look like shit!"

"So do you, asshole," Angelina replied. "But I didn't ask you to meet me here so we could exchange sweet compliments, Billy. We have a problem. Ben found out that your dad set us up. He knows everything and he dumped me. He refuses to speak to me or see me anymore. So yeah, that happened."

Billy thought a moment, "So is that why you're so upset, Angel? Cause Benny dumped you? What did the Boy Scout get feisty with you, call you a whore? You know I'd never treat you that way."

Billy could see his charm wasn't appreciated, "OK, calm down, Angel. I doubt he knows *everything* or even anything for that matter. So we lost our ability to keep tabs on him, distract him a little. That's really not a problem. He's in now and he's hooked. Pretty sure we have him exactly where we want him. You did your job, and you did it extremely well, Angel. Mission completed. You can drop the act and go back to being the lovely little she-devil we both know you are, and smile your way to just about anything you want in life."

Angelina didn't respond with words; she gave Billy a look that adequately expressed her hatred for him.

"Look, I'm meeting with my father for lunch in a few hours. He has something *important* he has to talk with me about, too. I hope he's not as worried as you about little Benny from Arkansas. I'll let him know what Ben told you and that your business with him is complete."

Billy quickly softened his tone, "You know, Angel, none of this would have happened if you'd just considered my offer last year."

Angel snapped back, "A marriage proposal is an offer!"

Billy smiled, "Hey, I thought we had something special. We would have made one hell of a team."

Angelina looked disgusted, "You mean you and your father would have made a great team with my father and his bank account! I'm good, Billy, trust me. I just wanted you and Dr. Evil to know what Ben told me and that our arrangement is finished."

Billy stood up and was about to leave when Angelina stopped him, "Billy, I'm going back to Boston and getting the hell away from all of you clowns. I gave my boss the news on Friday. But he was more concerned about any damage my leaving would do to his friendship with my father than giving a shit about what I was doing. Don't worry, I didn't tell him anything about Ben."

Billy started to walk away, but Angelina put her hand on his arm and gently pulled him back, "Billy, as a friend, an old friend. Leave Ben alone. He's a good man, maybe the last good man left in DC. Please don't ruin that. He was more than an assignment to me, I brought him home to meet my parents for God's sake!"

Billy laughed, "Goodbye, Angel. We'll always have Boston!"

Angelina shouted at the still laughing Billy's back as he was leaving the coffee shop, "You've underestimated him, Billy! He's won, he beat you all at your twisted little game!"

Billy stopped laughing and turned back to Angelina, "Oh, he'll fall in line, Angel. He'll fall right in line. Or he'll fall, in some other way."

Chapter 43

F ather and son sat across from each other at Fila, a high-end Italian restaurant on Pennsylvania Avenue in Washington, DC. Bradford had called Billy on Friday evening with the unusual request to meet him in town and in public. The two men were seldom seen together and when they were it was never close to where Bradford worked. Billy didn't think too much about the unusual circumstance around the request and did what his father asked of him. The interaction between father and son was strained. During Billy's childhood, Bradford's work kept him away from home most of the time and eventually he divorced Billy's mother and moved to DC. It wasn't until Billy had become a grown man that he moved from Boston to the capital to develop some type of relationship with his father. The two shared the same ambition and lack of ethics. Billy's confidence and charisma combined with determination to succeed had impressed his father, though he was much more aggressive, sometimes careless, and still had a great deal to learn from his father's perspective. Billy frequently behaved more like a fraternity brother and was far less refined and patient than his Washington-insider father.

"So, Dad, what brings us together on this fine Sunday afternoon? Not that I'm complaining, I've come to enjoy your company."

Bradford looked over his son with pride, "Well, son, I'm glad you feel that way because we'll be spending much more time together in the coming months."

Billy looked puzzled but waited for more from his father.

"I had a tough day at work Friday, son," Bradford chuckled. "It seems our little arrangement with Ted Seneca has been exposed, either by Ted himself or someone else. Either way, Ted has apparently left town. Maybe he went back to Buffalo, no one knows for sure yet. He's gone and so are our plans for Ben Gilsum to replace him."

Billy was panicking, "Dad, our little arrangement with Angel Rindge went south, too. She told me this morning that Ben knows everything. She's going back to Boston. That little…"

Bradford stopped his son short, "William, relax. None of that matters now. They can't touch us. I was able to talk my way out of any real trouble with my associates at the government, but we'll have to stop our operations here in town and elsewhere for a bit. We're going to have to disappear for a while."

Billy became angry, "Stop our operations? What the hell does that mean? We just walk away and let that little piece of shit take everything we've built?"

Bradford had expected this response, "Son, we got lucky here. We're not going to federal prison, or worse. We don't have to lose anything. We take what we've earned and we leave town. It'll be like a long vacation. In time, after all of this is forgotten we can start over. This is how it works, William. Trust me, I've done it more than once."

Billy didn't want to give up so easily, "Why don't we hire someone to go out to the woods and silence our friend from Arkansas?"

Bradford gave his son a disappointed stare, "Let me tell you something about that farmhouse in the woods where *our friend* is staying. There's an arsenal of weaponry there along with a man named Bryan Ashland who knows exactly how to use it. You send a couple of idiotic thugs to that house and any hope we have of a deal with the feds vanishes along with the thugs. Besides all of that, I have a few secrets there with *Mr. Black* that I'd rather keep secret. We're not gangsters, William. That's not how we handle our business. This is how things are done here and how you remain active for as long as I have."

Billy seemed to agree with his father, reluctantly.

Bradford continued, "I suppose it goes without saying our association with the Brothers of Herrad is concluded. I received a call from old man Tamworth's grandson asking to meet with his grandfather. I already know what he wants to discuss and I intend to save him the trouble. Our dealings with the old man are finished."

Billy replied to his father with an indifferent laugh.

"Son, you need to stop taking any of these things personally. Take your wins, and we've had plenty, with your losses. We haven't lost a thing here. We're leaving town with a king's ransom and no one is trying to take it from us or put us in jail for it. That's a hell of a win."

Billy nodded in agreement though he couldn't hide his anger.

Bradford ignored his son's irritation, "So the only thing left to discuss is where we're going. Our friend in Kansas City can help us get back on track fairly quickly. Maybe not here in DC, but he has unlimited resources in plenty of other lucrative locations."

Billy shook his head, "Kansas City? The fucking gateway to the west? If we're going west, I say Vegas. Sin City!"

Bradford laughed, "First of all William, the Gateway Arch is in St. Louis. And Sin City? Anyone who refers to Las Vegas as Sin City has never spent much time in Washington, DC!"

There was an awkward silence, broken up by Bradford who declared, "You know, you shouldn't swear so much William. It makes you sound like an amateur."

Billy ignored his father's criticism and went to work on his lunch that had just been delivered to the table.

Bradford continued, "What the hell, why not? Let's go have some fun in Las Vegas for a few weeks. You've earned it. But when I get bored there we're going to Kansas City, Missouri. Here's to the gateway to the west! The other one, in Kansas City," Bradford announced jokingly as he raised his glass, which was left hanging in the air alone.

"I'm not ready to retire just yet," Bradford concluded as he lowered his glass and began to eat his lunch.

Chapter 44

C huck Woodmere had worked for the company for just twelve years and had quickly moved up the ranks. He was young for a high-level manager, only in his mid-thirties, though his rapidly receding hairline and slightly overweight frame made him appear much older. Chuck seemed to have no compassion nor strong opinions about anything, at least he never shared them. Conversations with Chuck were, by design, quick, to the point, and over before the person on the other side could offer agreement, objection, or a response of any kind. He was a fiercely intelligent no-nonsense manager who learned to rely on the far more personable Ted, who he had hand-picked to be program manager to work directly with the staff in his group and to communicate just about everything that came down from upper management.

Chuck was a fair man and a good man but he made it a rule to distance himself personally from anyone he worked with. During his interview process at the company, Ben spent a short time with Chuck and one of the first things he said to Ben was that he didn't get social with his employees, ever. He didn't ask about anything personal, he didn't share anything personal, and he didn't care about anything personal. Aside from being impersonal, one of Chuck's signature moves at work was the dreaded-impromptu four o'clock staff meeting on a Friday preceding a holiday weekend, every holiday weekend. Until Ben's recent awakening, he and Chuck were alike in many ways and those traits were perfect for their positions at the company. Those personality traits were also part of the reason Ben was viewed as a candidate for accelerated promotion.

Ben noticed that Ted wasn't in the office again on Monday morning. His office door was shut and the light was off. Ted was always the first person in the office and his door was never closed. When Ben turned on his computer and opened his email, there was a meeting request for eight thirty from Chuck to the entire group with a subject line that read "Ted Seneca" and there was nothing more in the body of the request. *This cannot be good.* The facts that the meeting request included the entire group and that no one had approached Ben individually yet gave him some comfort, but he was concerned about what may have happened to his beloved boss.

There were whispers and quiet conversations about Ted in the large conference room when Ben arrived for the meeting.

"I heard he just vanished. Didn't tell anyone a thing, just took his personal items from his office and left Thursday. He's not returning anyone's calls."

Ben took a seat away from the rest of his coworkers and waited for Chuck to start the meeting.

Chuck came in and closed the door, "So, everyone I called you here this morning to share news about Ted Seneca. And hopefully, end any rumors that might be flying around the office. Some of you may know that Ted is no longer with us. He gave his resignation Friday morning."

There were whispers scattered throughout the room.

Chuck continued, "Now before you get started, he wasn't fired. He's not in any trouble, there isn't a layoff coming and all of you are perfectly secure here. Ted was a great manager and we'll miss him. He has his own personal reasons for leaving us and I'd ask that you all stop with the speculation that there's something sinister involved with his departure. There isn't."

Ben remained silent in the back of the room and though he knew there was a good chance this would happen, he wasn't fully prepared for it. Ted was more than just a great boss, he was Ben's only true friend at work. Ben couldn't imagine how things would be at the company without Ted. *And what about Mr. White?*

Chuck cleared his throat and continued speaking, "I will assume Ted's responsibilities here until we find a replacement." Chuck looked around the room and stopped his gaze on Ben Gilsum as he added, "Any of you who are interested in applying for the job can come and see me to discuss."

Ben looked away.

Chuck added, "Oh, and there's news to add from the government as well. One of our contacts has retired from his position and will no longer be active. Any projects you're currently working on with Mr. White will transfer to Ms. Green effective immediately."

There was a great deal of whispering and commotion throughout the room with that announcement and Chuck was quick to add over the voices, "There is absolutely no correlation between this news and Ted leaving us. Don't even go there. There is no there, people. Let it go."

Ben breathed a sigh of relief and tried to avoid eye contact with Chuck as he wrapped up the meeting.

"Unless any of you have questions and let me add that you don't, this meeting is concluded. Let's not allow any of this to be a distraction. We still have very important work to do."

For the rest of the day, Ben didn't speak to anyone in the office. People were buzzing all around him about all the possibilities and rumors of what could have happened, but Ben paid no attention to any of it. He spent most of the day wondering if Chuck would reach out to him to speak in private or worse if someone from the government would. Weeks would pass without any request for a private meeting, which was enough time for Ben to believe he was in the clear. *Ted held up his end of the deal.*

Chapter 45

Ben had stayed away from the Firehouse for a couple Thursdays, but as the excitement in his life seemed to calm down he was falling back into his old routine. The problem for Ben now was his old routine seemed to be terribly unsatisfying. *How the hell did I exist like this for two years?* He was a little concerned about going to a place where he might see Angelina, but there was someone else at the Firehouse he wanted to see again and hopefully see more often. Ben decided anything was better than another night alone in his small apartment watching baseball.

Once he made sure the coast was clear and Angelina wasn't there, Ben sat just off the bar hoping he might catch Patty for a quick word as she moved in and out of the area during her shift. He could see the employees staring at him and talking, but he didn't see Patty.

A waitress came to greet him and before she could ask him what he was having, Ben asked, "Is Patty in tonight?"

His waitress was new to the Firehouse and unsure if she could answer the question, "Um, I'm not sure…"

The bartender, who was familiar with Ben yelled from behind the bar, "Patty's not working tonight, honey."

Ben said thank you, clearly disappointed, and asked for a beer and a menu.

After sitting alone for just a moment, Ben heard laughs and hellos coming from the other side of the bar. *Oh no, please don't be.*

"Hey, you're not supposed to be here on your night off, lady!" Ben heard the bartender shout before he saw a smiling Patty coming over to join him.

He had only ever seen Patty working busy shifts at the Firehouse, running around the place, dressed for work and though she always looked nice, she was positively stunning now. Patty was quite a bit shorter than Ben; she had fair skin and long, dark-red hair she always pulled back while working. Tonight, it was down with a slight part near the middle. Her hair framed her pretty face, partially covering her right eye and slightly off her face on the left side. Her bright green eyes made it easy to maintain eye contact when she was talking and hard to look away when she wasn't. She caught Ben staring a few times and he couldn't help but laugh when Patty asked, "What?" every time she noticed.

Patty was wearing a tight black skirt with a black and blue, striped, form-fitting tank top, which was tucked in under a wide, black belt. The outfit highlighted Patty's thin, petite frame while accentuating her curves and it was working quite well for the newly single Ben Gilsum.

"Do you always come here on your nights off?" Ben asked as Patty sat across from him.

"Well, if I ever get another night off, I'll tell ya!" Patty answered.

The bartender couldn't help herself, "Don't count on it, honey!"

There was an awkward moment that followed and Patty wasn't sure if she should bring up Angelina, but wanted to break the silence. It was the obvious choice, "So, I'm sorry about you and Angel. You guys were so great together. I can't believe she moved back home!"

Ben pretended to not be completely taken by surprise that Angelina went back to Boston, "Thank you. Yeah, that was a surprise to me too. She loved her job here." *Well, at least one of her jobs!*

"Touchy subject, I'm sorry," Patty added.

"Don't be sorry, it's OK. I'm fine with it all. It just didn't work out. No hard feelings," Ben lied.

The two overcame another awkward moment and slowly began to talk more freely and openly about themselves. It was like a first date that started out difficult, but both were determined to not allow the spark to fade away. Eventually Ben gained enough confidence to ask Patty if she'd like to go on an actual date somewhere away from the Firehouse.

"As long as you promise not to take me to see any statues!" Patty responded with a laugh.

"Oh God, you heard about that?" Ben was slightly embarrassed. He remembered how that played out and was convinced it was a good move. But he had forgotten that his date that evening was paid to be there.

Ben was relieved at how well the night seemed to go and that Patty agreed to go out with him. He was at ease for the first time in weeks. There was something, however, he had to say before he allowed himself to go further. Ben had to be honest with Patty about his future which was unclear to him at the moment.

"Patty, I have to tell you something. I'm not really sure how to say this, but I want to be open with you. Things are still crazy for me. I don't know what's going to happen. I don't know where I'll even be in a week."

Patty didn't look troubled, "Tough nut to crack, Ben. You've always been such a tough nut to crack." She leaned over and gave Ben a kiss, "How about you relax for a minute and let things happen naturally. Nobody knows where they'll be in a week if we're being completely honest."

Chapter 46

Life had gone back to a deliberate pace for Ben over the past several weeks. He was seeing Patty frequently and volunteering at the Club on Saturdays. He had gone back to his routine of going to the Firehouse on Thursdays for dinner and drinks. He hadn't been given or taken on any assignments with the Brothers and still wasn't sure if he would go to his second Assembly as an official member. The Assembly was only one night away and Ben had been encouraged to go by his friend and mentor, Mr. James, but he had put off making a decision while he worked to get his life back on track. Now that things were mostly back to the way they had been before, Ben felt strongly that something in his life was missing. He never felt that way before, but things had changed in the past year and Ben had changed, too. He was struggling still to go back to the way he lived before meeting Angelina Rindge.

Work was slow again and Ben was taking on tasks directly from Chuck, which made the young intelligence analyst positively miserable. There was no social connection at the company for Ben, mostly due to his history of a complete lack of social skills or inability to make new friends. Though Ben had gained a more outgoing personality in recent months thanks to Angelina and Mr. James, he was unhappy and didn't bother to use his new social skills at work. Chuck and Ben were content to do their job quietly and leave each other to it. With the retirement of Mr. White, there was virtually no contact between people at Ben's level and the government. But Ben was informed that Ms. Green would be coming in to discuss the future with Ben and Chuck. It seemed as though the future which was once cloudy for Ben would be more in focus and Ben wasn't sure he was going to like it.

Ben had never seen Ms. Green before but had heard her voice on conference calls. She looked nothing like what he pictured when he finally met her in a small conference room with Chuck. Ben had imagined her to be older than she appeared in person, mostly due to her position in the government and level of experience and competence. Ms. Green was close to Ben's age, perhaps a couple of years older, still in her twenties. She was quite fit, with an athletic build, and short dark-brown hair. She looked and behaved like a soldier and Ben immediately assumed that like many people in federal law enforcement she was former military or police or both. Ms. Green was direct with her statements, never going off topic or offering what could be interpreted as an opinion on anything. There were no wasted statements in conversation with Ms. Green and she gave no impression of personality. She reminded Ben very much of Chuck in that regard. In fact, though Ben couldn't see it, the three people in the small conference room attending this meeting were in many ways the same.

Upon meeting Ms. Green and getting to know her from what little personality she showed, Ben assumed she was on some fast track through federal government law enforcement. He also assumed she was Ivy-League educated, former military, an officer maybe, or even Special Forces. This role was temporary and one of many she would take on along the way. She clearly looked and behaved like a person who belonged in the field, not in an office. Normally when Ben had such a strong read on a person as he did on Ms. Green, his assumptions were accurate. Ben was impressed with Ms. Green and admired her complete focus, discipline, and absolute respect for protocol. She was everything that Mr. White was not and the government couldn't have found a better person to pick up the pieces.

Ms. Green started the meeting, "I'm sure you have some idea why I'm here today. This meeting is going to be completely candid and before I get started, I want you to know the Government holds you in very high regard. We're proud of you, Ben. Chuck, as well as the management here at the company are proud of you." *Ted kept his word.* "Ben, we are aware of your investigation into the activities of Bradford and William Sullivan. Everything you discovered has been placed on record. At this time there will be no formal charges brought against them. Bradford has agreed to leave his position. If this outcome doesn't satisfy you, we can discuss now and perhaps the government will change its direction. This will be the only time we discuss this matter."

Ben looked at Chuck who motioned back to Ben to speak, "I have nothing to add, nor will I be doing any more investigating that isn't directly requested by Chuck or the government. I have no opinion about what should happen next with the Sullivans," Ben replied, wondering if he went too far with the last statement.

"Very well, Ben," Ms. Green answered. "Your response brings us to the next topic and I believe you've already answered our concern. You will not be conducting any investigation that hasn't been explicitly requested by your superiors at the company or your contacts at the government. If at any point you're unclear about what you should be doing, the protocol is to address your apprehension with Chuck. I think we can move on from that topic without further discussion."

Ms. Green paused as if waiting for a response from Ben or Chuck, but the two men knew not to question statements that began with the words "You will."

"Excellent," Ms. Green continued. "Ben, I'll remind you that we concern ourselves with fact and fact alone. We're given an assignment and we do our job, fully aware that what happens next is in the hands of someone else. We accept that and move on to the next assignment. We never become personally involved and should there be personal involvement the protocol is to stop immediately and disclose any involvement to Chuck. Are there any questions about what I just said?"

Ben remained silent.

"Excellent," Ms. Green added.

Ms. Green turned to Chuck indicating it was his turn to speak. "Very well, Ms. Green," Chuck took over. "Ben, now that we have a full understanding of what happened and what is expected going forward I want to repeat something Ms. Green said on behalf of the company. Job well done, young man! We are proud of you. To show you how pleased we are with what you've accomplished I'm prepared to offer you a promotion, effective immediately. We need someone to take over for Ted as program manager and you're the obvious choice. Let's finish out the week doing exactly what we're doing, but on Monday Ted's office will be your office. The transition will be seamless. You and I can discuss a few things next week but there's no concern from me or management you'll do an outstanding job. We've already cleared everything with the government and they welcome the move."

Ben was speechless. He knew that his name was on the short list for people to replace Ted. He and Ted had spoken about it several times when Ted discussed his retirement, but given his recent indiscretions, Ben was expecting to be outright fired instead of promoted. *Unless they're doing this to keep me quiet about White?*

The room had gone silent as Ben was lost in thought. He came to his senses and noticed Chuck and Ms. Green staring at him, expecting a response to what Chuck had just said. "I don't know what to say, I mean I wasn't expecting this to happen so soon. I guess we'll talk more about it on Monday," Ben finally answered.

Chuck laughed, "Yes Ben, I guess we will."

Chuck and Ms. Green weren't accustomed to subordinates saying no, so the fact that Ben was still thinking about the offer had not occurred to either of them.

"Gentlemen, our meeting is finished," Ms. Green concluded. "Ben, congratulations on your promotion. We'll be in touch and I'm looking forward to working with you. Chuck, thank you for your time. If you don't mind, I'd like to talk with Ben alone for a few moments."

Chuck was a bit puzzled but didn't question the request, "Of course, Ms. Green. It's always a pleasure speaking with you. Ben will show you out when you've finished your conversation." Chuck left the small conference room and closed the door.

"As you know in our profession Ben, nothing is ever off the record. But what I'm about to say to you is off the record. I sense the confusion in you about what just happened. Ben, you're an extremely valuable asset to the company and to the government. The courage you showed and your ultimate decision to do what was right in the face of losing everything has not gone unnoticed. In fact, it's the reason you and I are having this conversation. I want to clear up any confusion you may be experiencing, off the record of course."

Ben was intrigued, but remained silent as Ms. Green continued, "First, you may be wondering why I'm not here with an armed escort watching as you're taken away in handcuffs. Ben, as you know, before we conduct any search of individuals or organizations we obtain court approval. Since we had been granted such approval to investigate the Brothers of Herrad, what you did was not a violation of the law. A clear violation of protocol, which we discussed, but we're covered legally. Second, since there was no personal gain for you, and your motives though questionable were not to harm anyone, we were able to exercise discretion in your situation. Third, and perhaps most important, you put an end to something embarrassing happening within both of our organizations. You handled that part perfectly, Ben."

Ben was still confused and Ms. Green could see it.

"Ben, you're still not satisfied. Please speak freely. We're off the record. Truly Ben, off the record."

Ben wasn't comfortable speaking, but he had to say what was on his mind, "Ms. Green, with respect, you don't owe me this promotion. I broke the rules. I get what you're saying and I appreciate the fact that I'm still here. That's one thing, but there's more. I know I'm not supposed to question what happens next, but this one is different." Ben hesitated and nearly changed his mind about speaking, but decided to let his trouble be known, "Why are the Sullivans walking?" He regretted it the moment he asked. Ben expected Ms. Green to remind him of protocol, "We do our job fully aware that what happens next is in the hands of someone else," and return to her cold demeanor, but she surprised him.

"I suspected that was bothering you and I understand your concern. You and I are more alike than you know Ben." *Like hell we are!* "Ben, I mean every word about you being an asset. You're special, Ben, and we don't want to lose you. I'm not just telling you that so you'll go off and be a good patriot. We expect big things from you. And as far as the Sullivans are concerned, I agree with you. They're getting off entirely too easy but that's out of our hands. Bradford Sullivan has been a true patriot during most of his very long career. He has friends in high places and to be perfectly candid, going after him would cast a shadow over both your company and my department. The combination of those two things was apparently enough for my superiors to end this as it is."

Ms. Green could see that Ben was understanding things better, but she added a bit more to ease his mind, "Ben, we do great work here. Maybe these bad guys are slipping away while we look the other way, but sometimes we have to do what's best for the government. We can't afford to allow something simple to jeopardize our ability to continue to do great work." *There it is!*

Ms. Green stopped and studied Ben for a moment, "Ben, I think we're done here. Before you show me out, I'd like to add one thing off the record. Take the promotion Ben, you deserve it. You're the right person for it. Stop worrying about this immediately, you're in the clear. The file is sealed, and no one is ever going to reopen it."

Chapter 47

B en decided he would continue his involvement with the Brothers of Herrad and attend the Assembly this month. The meeting would be a welcome distraction to take his mind off of work for a while, since his head was still buzzing over the thought of being program manager. Ben was worried about how awkward things would be if the Sullivans were there, but believed Mr. James had kept his word and he wouldn't see them. As Ben put on his only suit, the thought occurred to him that if he accepted the new position at work, and it seemed they weren't considering the possibility he wouldn't, he would need to buy some new clothes. *Dress for the job you didn't really want?*

For the first time, Ben was uncharacteristically late, struggling to straighten his tie in the car. *I hate these fucking things!* As he walked up to the entrance of the building, Ben looked around and noticed there were very few cars parked on the sides of the streets. There had never been so many empty spaces so close and there was only one light on in the front lobby. The large hall was dark, and the building looked empty from the outside. *This is the first Wednesday of the month, right?* The front door was not only unlocked it was open slightly, so Ben went inside and closed the door behind him. There seemed to be no one in the building. His heart was already racing about the possibility of seeing the Sullivans and this was positively creepy.

With a look down the dark hallway leading to the meeting hall, Ben called out, "Hello!"

No one answered.

He took a few steps in the dark not knowing where the light switch was but thought he heard a noise in the meeting hall and stopped short. The dark, old building with the musty smell was silent and Ben was getting nervous chills.

"Is anyone here?" he called out and waited, but there was no answer so he took a few more steps in the dark. *This is ridiculous, there's no one here! What am I doing...*

"BANG!" A loud crashing sound came from the meeting hall and Ben froze in his tracks.

What the hell! Ben's heart nearly jumped from his chest when the door to the meeting hall swung open! A scruffy-looking dog had somehow wandered into the building and got spooked from knocking an empty chair off the stage. It came running out toward the front door. Relieved but still shaking, Ben opened the door and let the panicked stray dog out into the street. It was difficult to tell who was more scared by the incident, Ben or the poor mangy mutt.

The petrified Ben Gilsum was ready to get the hell out of there but took one last look around and noticed a sheet of paper on a small table that looked like a handwritten letter. He picked it up, hands still shaking, and realized it was addressed to him.

Dear Ben,

I'm pleased that you've decided to attend tonight's activities, but as you can see the Assembly has been canceled. I do apologize for not being there in person to deliver this message and for not informing you sooner of the following. I'm not doing well Ben and I had to have this letter delivered by a driver. I had hoped to be feeling better by this evening, but I'm afraid that isn't the case.

Ben, we've disbanded our group in Washington, DC. Bradford and Billy Sullivan as well as a few close associates of theirs have been removed from the Brothers completely and as a precaution, we've determined it was prudent to close this lodge. Remaining members have been given the opportunity to seek membership elsewhere or perhaps with another organization. There are many terrific opportunities locally where a man with the proper motivation can do great things for the community.

My intention was to speak with you in private to discuss your future with us. Unfortunately, due to my current state of health, I've been unable to contact you. Ben, I hope you will remain patient while I work to get my well-being in order. Should something happen, a close associate will provide you with further detail and of my intentions.

Please continue to trust yourself son, and spend the rest of your life earning that trust.

With my sincere apologies

Jim Tamworth

Ben was unsure what to think about the letter. *Was there no one who could have called me, or sent an email? A text message? Why couldn't Mr. James have sent his driver to my house before I got dressed and drove to Alexandria to attend a meeting for a group that no longer existed? "Membership elsewhere?" "Close this lodge?" Did the Brothers have other lodges outside DC and why didn't I know that? Why is that not an option for me? Am I out? And since when does Mr. James refer to himself by his actual name?* Ben had never heard him or anyone else refer to Mr. James as Jim Tamworth.

Ben took another look around and sighed. *I don't even know what I'm doing here.*

Chapter 48

Ben had difficult news he needed to share with Patty, who was working on Thursday at the Firehouse. It had taken him several weeks to make up his mind, but he was finally sure about what he would do. Now he had to tell Patty. The two were seeing each other more, but it was hard for either to gauge how serious things were due to Ben's unwillingness to fully commit. He'd told Patty in the beginning about his uncertainty and she was fully aware of how difficult it was to penetrate Ben's shell. Patty knew the man behind the invisible shield was worth the wait and she ignored his warning. In a short time, the two had developed strong feelings for one another. Patty knew how to manage Ben's guarded nature quite well. She had coined the phrase "tough nut to crack," as she was raised in a household by a father who exhibited that trait long before she met Ben Gilsum. Patty was good for Ben and it didn't take long for him to figure it out.

Patty was making her rounds and passing by Ben as often as she could to say, "Hey babe!" with a wink or smile as she flew by. She was in a great mood and Ben felt increasingly terrible about what he needed to tell her with each pass. *I know this is the right decision!* Ben intended to wait at the bar for Patty's shift to end, which was late and much later than Ben typically stayed on Thursdays.

"Honey, are you waiting around for Patty?" the bartender asked.

"Actually I am," Ben replied.

"Oh honey, it's gonna be late. It's crazy in here!"

Ben nodded in agreement but he planned to wait as long as it took to have a private conversation with the adorable redhead who was buzzing around the bar making everyone smile. *I really don't want to do this!*

The bartender eventually told Patty that Ben was waiting for her. She hadn't noticed the time he normally went home had passed.

"Are you waiting for me, Ben Gilsum?" Patty asked with a devilish smile as she found time for a quick visit between working her tables.

"Yeah, if you can I'd like to talk with you after you get out," Ben answered.

Patty knew something was wrong and immediately began to worry. "Hold on, I may be able to get out early," Patty said as she vanished into the kitchen.

Patty convinced a waitress whose shift was ending before closing time to stay and cover for her so she could leave with Ben. "OK, babe, I'm off the hook. Give me about twenty minutes and I'm yours," Patty said as she vanished again.

Ben waited as Patty finished up her shortened shift and eventually sat next to him at the bar.

"You ready?" she asked as she put her hand on his leg.

"Have fun you two!" the bartender shouted as they walked out. "I absolutely love them!" she admitted to the few patrons still sitting at the bar.

"So, Ben, what are we doing?" Patty asked as they slowly walked down the sidewalk toward both of their cars.

"Patty, there's something I need to talk to you about. I had to tell you the moment I knew, I couldn't wait any longer," Ben replied.

Patty was already worried and she was getting upset. "You and Angel getting back together?" she asked, showing some insecurity even though Angelina had already left for Boston.

No chance! Ben answered, "Oh, God no, it's not that. Please don't ever think that's going to happen Patty. I'll never go back to her and I'd never leave you for her, anyway."

A weak smile had crept back to Patty's face, but she was still worried, "Then what's wrong, Ben?"

Ben stopped walking and turned to face Patty on the sidewalk. "Patty, I'm leaving," was all he could say, and he had a hard time believing the words as he spoke them aloud for the first time.

"You're leaving what?" Patty asked nervously.

"I'm going back to Arkansas," Ben managed and looked away.

Patty waited for more, but Ben stared off into the street. She knew not to push too hard and stepped around Ben, placing herself in the path of his gaze. "Ben, you're scaring me. Are you in any kind of trouble? Is everything OK?" she asked.

Ben refocused his attention on Patty, touched that at this moment she showed more concern for him than herself, "Yeah, everything is fine Patty. I just need to get out of here. This city, these people. I don't belong here. I don't think I've ever belonged here. I need to go home."

Patty looked at Ben and waited for him to finish telling her what he was feeling. Hoping to get more from him, but he stopped talking. "Babe, that's one of the first things I noticed about you, and I loved it right away. You don't belong here," Patty said as a tear fell from her cheek.

Ben was crushed by guilt as he watched her tearing up. She never tried to tell him he was wrong nor did she try to change his mind. He'd almost wished she would talk him out of leaving at that moment, but he knew he had to go home.

"Patty, I'm so sorry. I wish this wasn't happening, but I have to do this."

Patty didn't respond, only nodding her head. She was crying a little more and Ben was starting to tear up as well.

Ben was realizing how strong his feelings for Patty were, "This doesn't have to be the end for us, I mean you could come see me in Decatur. You could meet my parents." Ben almost couldn't believe what he was saying, but he meant every word. He wanted Patty to meet his mother. He wanted his mother to know how special Patty was and he didn't care what their house looked like or what his neighborhood looked like.

"I could come back here and visit you, too," Ben said. He could not stop himself from crying with the sudden rush of emotion he was feeling, the likes of which he hadn't felt since the day he left his mother to come to Virginia.

The young couple didn't speak for a while, both of them staring at each other and crying on the sidewalk outside the Columbia Firehouse.

"You really want me to meet your parents?" Patty asked, managing a smile with sad eyes and a tear-soaked face.

Ben felt a sense of relief and his own tears fell faster. "I really want you to," Ben replied as he moved closer and wrapped his arms around Patty.

Chapter 49

Ben gave a two-week notice to a completely shocked Chuck Woodmere Monday morning when Ben was supposed to be moving into Ted's office. However, Chuck denied the notice and made Ben's departure from the company effective immediately. The company never accepted notice of any kind due to security concerns. Ben felt a sense of relief as he was escorted to his office to collect his belongings and then immediately to the front door, which he no longer had any ability to open from the outside.

The former intelligence analyst could hear his coworkers whispering as he moved past them on his way out. No one knew he quit and Ben could sense everyone thought he was caught up in the same wicked deeds that were rumored to have led to Ted's exit and Mr. White's "retirement." Ben didn't care, he was happy he wouldn't be reporting directly to Chuck Woodmere anymore, a thought that had kept him up at night. Ben was also not willing to take on the role of program manager. He was content in his position and had everything he wanted financially. Ben had little ambition to take on more work, spend more time at work, and experience the stress and pressure of being a manager for what he felt was a relatively small amount of financial gain.

Ben also notified his landlord that he would not be renewing his lease in the coming months. Bryan Ashland was disappointed to be losing his perfect tenant, but told the young man he would tear up their contract and Ben could leave anytime he wanted. Ben was not to worry about the lease agreement. Bryan told Ben he was proud of him for having the courage to do what he had done and now that it was over he didn't blame him for walking away. Ben should walk away with his head held high. *How the hell does he know anything about any of that?*

Over the next couple of weeks, Ben spent as much time with Patty as he could and also looked for a job near Decatur.

The latter proved to be difficult for the young man. Ben exhausted all other possibilities before finally contacting Human Resources at the plant where his father worked, along with most other fathers he knew as a kid growing up in Decatur. The HR Manager was someone from his high school and she was thrilled to hear from him. There was a new position they were having a hard time filling, and she said Ben would be the perfect fit. After a few phone interviews with a couple different managers, he was hired and it was determined Ben would return to Decatur in two weeks to work at the plant. As a cost estimator, Ben would help management determine how new projects would affect the plant financially as well as monitor current processes to be sure they were the most efficient.

Ben tried to warn the HR Manager he wasn't an accountant and she laughed at him.

"Ben Gilsum! You're the smartest person that ever went to Decatur High School. You'll figure it out, darlin'!"

Chapter 50

Ben had taken care of every aspect of moving back to Decatur except for one. He wasn't sure how his mother would take the news as he prepared to make his typical Wednesday phone call home. Ben knew his mother wanted him to get out of Decatur and see the world, despite how much she would hate not having him close. He was as afraid the news of moving back might leave her disappointed and he was equally afraid to share the news of his taking a job at the plant. He took a deep breath and waited as the phone rang once, twice, "Hello Ben, how you doing, baby?"

There were the typical questions and answers. Not much had changed back home, not much ever changed back home. Ben's father shouted his typical "Hi, Ben!" from his spot in front of the television in the next room. Ben was grateful there were no questions about Angelina or his love life. His mother knew him well enough to leave that alone and wait for him to come to her if he needed to.

"Mom, I have some really big news to tell you and Dad," Ben finally announced.

Mrs. Gilsum was hoping her son was about to tell her all about a rekindled romance with Angelina and perhaps even an engagement, but the news she got was far more exciting.

"Oh, honey, honey get in here quick, honey!" Mrs. Gilsum shouted to Mr. Gilsum who came rushing into the kitchen with visions of something awful happening.

Mr. Gilsum ran into the kitchen and slid to a stop on his socks when he saw Mrs. Gilsum was still on the phone, "What the hell's the matter in here!?"

Mrs. Gilsum shouted, "Ben's coming home. Ben is coming home!" she repeated cheerfully.

"Son, you coming for a visit?" Mr. Gilsum asked loud enough so Ben could hear him over the phone.

"No, honey, he's moving back to Decatur!" Mrs. Gilsum answered with glee.

"Well now, why's he gone and done that for?" Mr. Gilsum asked..

"Don't you question a blessing honey, and there's more," Mrs. Gilsum said. "He's got himself a job at the plant and he starts in twelve days!"

Mr. Gilsum looked even more puzzled than when he entered the room, "Well shit, what the hell's he done that for!"

Mrs. Gilsum had lost her patience with her husband, "Get outta here with that talk, go on back to your TV. Scoot, old man!" she shouted.

Ben felt he owed his mother an explanation, even though she didn't need it and wasn't about to ask for one, "Mom, I know you wanted me to go out into the world and do amazing things, but most of what I found out here was not very amazing at all. I think I picked the wrong place to start."

Mrs. Gilsum was having none of it, "Baby, you don't need to tell me anything else. You're a grown man and a damn good one. The only thing I want is for you to be happy and if coming back here makes you happy then I don't want you to be anywhere else. Besides, son, you've got your whole life to figure out what happens next. You've worked hard and with that comes the opportunity to try new things, make mistakes, and then go try other new things. There's no chance you could ever disappoint me, Ben. No chance. Someday if you wanna tell me all about what you found out there that made you want to come back, I'll be ready to listen. Your father has always been one to see the bad in everything and that makes him never trust anyone and never try new things. He goes right to the negative, just like he did tonight. But you, Ben, you're special. You see the good in everything and in everyone and that makes you work so hard to be part of it all and do what you can to take care of those around you. I can only imagine a person like you, surrounded by all the evils that Washington, DC, has to offer. Baby, I'm surprised you lasted as long as you did there!"

Chapter 51

Things were going well at his new job and Ben's old classmate from HR was right. He figured it out, and he figured it out quickly. Ben had spent less than a month at the plant and his input was already saving thousands of dollars. He was working with people he had known for years and was told repeatedly how much he changed since leaving Decatur.

"Silent Ben went off to DC and came back a new man!"

Ben had changed and his mother was the first to notice and tell him how happy she was to see him more confident and loquacious, "Baby, I don't know what happened out there and I know you've been hurting inside, but as far as I can tell you came home to us full of nothing but energy and happiness. I've had to stop and thank the Lord above every day since you've been back."

Though he was feeling a renewed sense of energy since coming home and he was doing well at work, Ben had the feeling again that something was missing. *So is this how I'm going to spend the next forty years?* After a few weeks, he was looking into ways he could begin volunteering again and working with kids in the area like he had at the club in Alexandria. All the resources he found were linked to specific churches and religious groups, and Ben wasn't interested in being part of a religious organization. There were scouting troops and parks and recreation sports he could try to be a part of, but they were mostly staffed by volunteers who had children in the various programs. Ben wasn't sure how they would respond to a person without a child showing up to join.

Every day on his way to the plant, Ben passed an old church building that was boarded up around the windows and doors. The building appeared to be in good shape structure wise and there was a good deal of land around the old church that someone was keeping clean and neat. It was a white, split-entry building with four big, stained-glass windows on each side of the top floor. The windows were either hidden under boards or missing completely. The building was a plain, large, rectangle-shaped construction with a steeple built into the roof on one side, the cross had been removed from the top of the steeple. There were stairs outside on the steeple side of the building that led to the top floor and a door on one of the sides beneath the stained-glass windows that allowed entry to the bottom floor from the outside. The old church sat on a couple acres of well-maintained fields surrounded by woods. Ben remembered it being abandoned back when he lived in town, but no one ever cut the grass or took care of any maintenance. The property was for sale and Ben decided he would ask his father what he knew about it. Mr. Gilsum typically knew everything about the business of the town and Ben was sure he could learn the entire history of the church by asking him. The two men were commuting to work together daily, which was sometimes awkward due to lack of conversation. Mr. Gilsum, like his son, was never one for conversation. *Tough nut to crack.*

One morning on the way to the plant, Ben asked his father what he knew about the old church as they passed it and Mr. Gilsum did not let him down.

"That church was full of life when I was a boy, but it was Catholic and most folk around here are Baptist as you know. They managed to keep it goin til some twenty years ago and then the Catholics sold it to a retired

194

Navy Seal of all people back when you were just a baby. That Navy Seal actually lived in the building and opened up a karate school there that only lasted a couple years before he couldn't keep it going anymore and had to sell it. The town bought it off him and held it for years and years while they couldn't decide what the heck to do with it. They sold it just a couple months ago to some feller from out of town who gave them a truckload of cash for it to do nobody knows what with. I'm thinking he's from Missourah. Seen his car there a couple times with Missourah plates. There was all sorts of rumors, but that's all they were. That Missourah feller cleaned it up real nice, inside and out so people were happy enough about that to not ask too many questions. It looks real good now, but he boarded it all up and stuck a for sale sign on it just about when you come back to town. He's had two or three offers too but turned them all down flat. No one knows what he's up to."

The Gilsum family sat down for dinner that evening and the mood was happy. Mrs. Gilsum was still buzzing about having her son home. Ben had been thinking about the old church all day and decided to share an idea he had with his parents.

"Mom, you know that old church out near North Main that's been empty for years?" Ben asked.

"Yes, that's been closed up since you were a boy. What about it?" Mrs. Gilsum answered.

Ben perked up, "Well, I was talking with Dad about it this morning and it's for sale. You know there's not a whole lot for the poor kids around here to do besides go to church or school right? When I was in Virginia I did some work at a Boys and Girls Club with some of the local kids. They'd come and play sports, or games with other kids. Some of them would just come and hang out. It was something for them to do and stay out of trouble."

Ben's mother interrupted, "Oh, baby, we don't really have that much trouble here in Decatur. It's pretty quiet around here."

Ben nodded, "Well, that's true, but there's still a lot of kids that need something to do right? And plenty of families that can't afford much. I was thinking, why not buy that old building and turn it into a place like a Boys and Girls Club?"

Ben's father answered, "Now, Ben, I told you the feller that owns that church paid a ridiculous amount of money for it, and he's turned down quality offers already. I don't know what they're paying you at the plant, but I'm sure you can't afford that place son."

"I saved a few dollars over the last couple of years and I've been maximizing my 401K contribution. I can come up with a decent down payment and maybe if I talk to the owner and explain what my plans are, he may work with me. I could live there like the old Navy Seal did and pay it off like a mortgage, Dad."

Mr. Gilsum laughed at his extremely intelligent yet wildly naive son, "Unless you got a million dollars hidden in your mattress he ain't even gonna talk to you, Ben. The world don't work that way, boy."

Mrs. Gilsum had heard enough, "Baby, why don't you write a letter to the realtor and ask them to share it with the owner. You come up with enough cash and add some of your passion and charm to a beautifully worded letter, and who knows what might happen."

Mr. Gilsum wasn't finished, "Now, wait a minute you two! Come up with enough cash? Ain't we gonna even talk about if this is a good idea or not? What if you do spend all your retirement money and savings on this thing and by some miracle this feller sells it to you, *at a loss*, and then your whole idea flops? What then? Well, you'll be sittin in that old church all alone, broke and half starved, wishin you'd listened to your father just one time. That's what!"

Ben chose to ignore his father and with his mother's encouragement, he wrote an offer letter to the realtor for the old church building. He pulled together an impressive amount of cash for the offer, but it was still well below what the seller was asking. He wrote what he felt was a passionate appeal to the owner, describing his life as a poor child growing up in Decatur. Ben explained in his letter how his vision for the old building would have done so much to improve his quality of life if it existed when he was a child.

"Well, Mom, I sent the letter. Nothing we can do now but wait right?"

Chapter 52

atty had decided she would wait for Ben to call before reaching out to him in Arkansas. Both were a little skeptical about a long distance relationship but neither was willing to give up. They decided to see how things went and talk about the future later. Ben called the moment he was at home and given a minute alone by his adoring and ecstatic mother. The two spoke on the phone every night for weeks and Ben eventually found the courage to ask his parents what they thought about a visit from his friend from Virginia.

"But, baby, I thought you broke up with her?" Mrs. Gilsum asked, confused now why he left Angelina back in DC alone.

Ben quickly realized he'd never told his parents about his new girlfriend to avoid questions about his old girlfriend and keep things simple.

"Mom, that's Angel. She went back to Boston. It didn't work out with her," Ben answered, hoping his mother would leave it alone. "I'm talking about Patty now, she and I started seeing each other shortly after Angel went home."

"Who the heck is Patty?" Mrs. Gilsum snapped. *Ah shit.*

"Mom, it's not that complicated. Patty and I were friends for a long time before I even met Angel," Ben lied. His mother knew it. "Then when things didn't work out with Angel, she and I started dating." *No way that's gonna fly.*

"So, baby, are you telling me it was you that sent Angel off? Son, did you cheat on that sweet girl? I know I raised you better than that!" Mrs. Gilsum shouted. *Sweet girl my ass!*

Ben stopped his mother quickly, "Mom! No, it wasn't like that at all! And I don't wanna talk about Angel. Please?"

Ben softened his tone as soon as he realized he raised his voice to his mother, "Mom, Angel wasn't sweet at all. I'd really appreciate it if you would trust me and just leave it at that. Patty is the one who helped me get over Angel. She's the reason I'm so happy and different now."

Ben's mother reluctantly gave in to her son's wishes, "OK, baby, I'll drop it. For now. But someday you're gonna tell me all about it. I'll be here when you're ready. And if this Patty person is a friend of yours, baby, she's always welcome here. Of course she can come and visit. Some time."

The young couple planned Patty's visit to Decatur for the coming fall, after things cooled down a little in the south and also at the Gilsum house. Ben didn't have the heart to tell Patty his mother already hated her or that she blamed her for breaking up her only son from the girl of *her* dreams.

Chapter 53

"**B**aby, you got a letter from that realty company about the church," Mrs. Gilsum said as she handed an envelope to Ben while he was watching baseball highlights with his father.

Ben was nervous as he opened it up but could barely contain himself while he read the letter in front of his parents.

"Well, what does it say?" Mrs. Gilsum asked eagerly.

"They're prepared to accept my offer, but the owner of the property wants to meet me there at the building on Wednesday evening to talk about the details," Ben answered.

"Like the fact that you don't have enough money? Maybe he'd like you to sell puppies, son." Mr. Gilsum added, not taking his eyes off the television.

Wednesday after work Ben put on his one and only suit and prepared to leave his parents' house to meet the owner of the old church building. *I feel like I should be carrying something, like a briefcase or documents of some kind.* The drive alone in his Jeep gave him time to think and speak aloud to himself about Patty and his parents' reluctance to accept her. "It's like it was before I left home! No one is ever good enough. Well, Patty is perfect but they think Angel is...An actual Angel! What an absolute joke!"

Ben continued protesting aloud as he turned onto North Main Street but something diverted his attention. He caught a glance of a very familiar dark-blue Mercedes S-Class Sedan pulling out of a gas station and heading in the opposite direction. "Is that? No! It can't be! Billy's car was black. I'm sure of it, it was black…"

Still rattled by the site of the Mercedes, Ben tried to calm himself as he pulled up to the old church building, "OK, you're here Ben. Get your shit together! Surely someone in this town has an S-Class." *Really? A $90,000 car? In Decatur?* He parked his Jeep in front of the old building and noticed there was a brown, Lexus LS 500 there with Missouri plates. *Beautiful car, terrible color!*

The building was well lit inside and out so Ben walked up the steeple-side stairs and knocked a couple times on the door and then opened it up, "Hello."

There was a man inside, alone, who appeared to be in his forties. He was a tall, thin man with blonde hair and glasses, wearing jeans with a dress shirt and a sports jacket with no tie. He had sneakers on his feet and Ben immediately thought of his old friend back in Virginia, Mr. James and smiled.

"Yes. Ben, do come inside. I'm pleased to meet you, my name is Doug. Doug Tamworth," the man said as he reached out for a handshake. *Tamworth?*

"My grandfather sends his warmest regards. He wanted to be here, but he's still not quite over his bout with pneumonia. He's feeling much better and at this point, they're just being cautious due to his age. I'd hoped he'd fly out to Kansas City and make the drive with me, but I drove here alone. Not a bad ride, just about three hours."

Ben was taken back, "Mr. James is your grandfather? Who owns this building?" Ben asked as his nerves started to build.

Doug answered, "Yes, Ben, Jim Tamworth is my grandfather. He bought this property a short time ago and I'm here to discuss the future of this place with you, the new owner." *You have got to be kidding me!*

Ben was still confused and wasn't sure what to say next. Doug continued, "I brought some documents we'll review and you can sign. Everything will be handled promptly by my office in Kansas City. You'll see it's all been taken care of. I also have several things to offer you from my grandfather that we'll discuss shortly. Ben, you've made a hell of an impression on my grandfather and you'll soon discover how generous a man Jim Tamworth can be."

"I'm not sure I understand; this building is for sale. The sign out front? There've been offers. I made an offer to buy…"

Doug interrupted, "For legalities only Ben, and appearances. I've taken the sign down." Doug pointed to the realty sign on a table nearby, "There will be a purchase and sale for the transfer of ownership. All for the fee of one dollar, Mr. Gilsum. We'll go over the details in a moment."

Ben's heart was beating faster, "Shouldn't there be a lawyer here or something?"

Doug laughed, "Well Ben, I am a lawyer. I've been handling my grandfather's interests for twenty years. I also handle most of his communication. As I'm sure you're aware, my grandfather doesn't use email or text. In fact, the old man refuses to buy a cellphone."

The two men sat at a table to review the documents Doug brought to the meeting. Ben was still hesitant but signed what he needed to in order to acquire the property. He was stunned, but slowly came to his senses. The young man's mind was racing and thinking about the "several other things" Mr. James had to offer. *What exactly is going on here?* Ben let that go momentarily and focused on the old church. Each time he began to tell Doug about his plans for the building, Doug would quickly change the subject to the next document, telling Ben they would discuss that in a moment, assuring him that once he became the legal owner he had free sovereignty to do what he wished with the building. Doug insisted that Ben review all the documentation and understand before he signed.

The last document was reviewed and signed and Doug stood up. Ben stood as well, and the men shook hands.

"Congratulations, Mr. Gilsum. Ben, walk with me a moment. We'll take a quick look at your new property," Doug requested. Ben followed Doug as they toured the old building which included an apartment added by the Navy Seal who once owned the place and made his home there. The building was in terrific condition and Doug pointed out some repairs that were made under his grandfather's ownership to be certain everything was up to code. *I'm not gonna need to fix a thing!* Doug was carrying a briefcase with him the entire time and when they made it to the last room of the tour, he placed it on a table and opened it.

"Ben, I know you have a thousand questions and you're still not comfortable with all of this. Let me assure you again, this is all legal and proper. My grandfather is very much aware, as am I, that you are a man of extreme moral integrity. You're under no obligation to accept these other items from my grandfather and your decision will have no bearing on the ownership of this property. No matter what you decide, you own this place, Ben. You can do anything you want here. Do you understand?"

Ben still didn't understand, but he nodded and said yes.

Doug continued, "Well, Ben, since today is the first Wednesday of the month, we have a few orders of business to attend to, Brother."

Ben was getting nervous again as Doug pulled an old leather-bound book and a ring from his briefcase. *Is that...*

"You may recognize this, Brother Gilsum. You first saw it a few months ago at your initiation. This book contains some original texts written by Herrad of Landsberg that my grandfather says he claimed during his time with the Freemasons. You might also remember seeing this ring once or twice?" Doug held out a gold ring with the letter M on the bezel.

"That's Mr. White's ring!" Ben declared.

"You would be the third person to wear this ring since it was given to my grandfather by the Freemasons. My grandfather was the first and then, yes it was worn by Bradford Sullivan who was gracious enough to return it to my office recently following his departure from the Brothers. And now, if you'll have it, this ring is yours."

Ben stared at the ring and said aloud, "M?"

Doug answered, "M for Melchior, the Third King, witness of the birth of God on Earth, representative of all humankind."

Ben stopped Doug, "I would own this ring?" he asked.

Doug answered, "Ben, I'm here to transfer ownership of this building to you and to inform you that you've been chosen to be the next Worshipful Master of the Brothers of Herrad. With that title comes possession of this book and this ring. We hope that you'll do all the things you plan for this building, and start a new lodge here in Decatur, but that's entirely up to you."

"Worshipful Master?" Ben asked. "I don't even know if I'm a member anymore. The Brothers were disbanded back in Alexandria."

Doug replied, "Ben if you would, please open the book and look at the last few pages."

Ben opened the book and noticed there were pages containing lists of names associated with different cities and lodges. There were dozens of lodges scattered all over the country.

Doug continued, "Ben, we're a bit larger than I think you were aware. We closed just that one lodge due to the behavior of its leadership. We didn't want to take any chances of their activities continuing. I apologize for the way things developed in Virginia, but we had to be absolutely certain of your intentions. You didn't disappoint, Ben. You've never disappointed."

"I don't know how to be Worshipful Master. I barely know how to be a member," Ben admitted.

"Ben if you take possession of these items, I'll return in a couple months, when you're ready, and we can work on that. Go ahead with your plans for this place as you intended. We'll work on the rest in due time. I will need an answer before I leave here tonight, though. And then there's more I'd like to share with you," Doug said as he removed an envelope from his briefcase.

"More!?" Ben replied. "Wait, though. So if I walk away from the Brothers, I still get to keep this place?" Ben asked.

"Absolutely, Ben, and there will be no hard feelings. We're grateful for what you did in Virginia. Consider this a token of my grandfather's appreciation. You saved something of immeasurable value to him from becoming corrupted."

Ben took a moment to think about everything that was happening. He considered how exciting it was to be part of the Brothers of Herrad and how much he valued his friendship with Mr. James. "You know, we're in the Bible belt right?" Ben asked. "I mean, these people may not take kindly to these stories of the Three Wise Men being portrayed as lawyerly types for ancient deals between God, the devil, and man."

Doug laughed, "Take a closer look at that book, Mr. Gilsum. We're all over the Bible belt and we do a lot of great things down here. We have an exceptionally diverse membership."

Ben took a deep breath and extended his hand to Doug, "Mr. Tamworth, I accept your offer. I'll do it, but I have to tell you I'm gonna need help here."

Doug shook Ben's hand, "You'll have all the help you need Mr. Gilsum. Remember, I'm only a three-hour drive away."

Doug paused before moving back to his briefcase and looked at Ben who was clearly still nervous. "Ben, relax, you're a part of something special. No regrets my friend!" *Where have I heard that before?!*

Ben was taken aback by the last two sentences spoken by Doug Tamworth. The words echoed in Ben's mind and instantly reminded him of what Billy Sullivan said the first time the two men met back in Virginia in Ben's apartment. The tone and look on Doug's face was identical to Billy's, and Ben instantly felt even more uneasy about what was happening.

Doug sensed Ben's apprehension, but continued on, "As I mentioned before, you'll be the third leader of the Brothers of Herrad. This is very exciting for us because you'll be the first leader who truly takes on the influence of the Third King. Most of us have determined my grandfather is of the First King, ruled by truth and justice. He had the conviction to leave the Freemasons because he was convinced they'd become corrupt. We've all decided that Bradford Sullivan was influenced a bit too much by the Second King, as I'm sure you would agree. And now you Ben. Your empathy and compassion toward those around you. You are surely a person influenced by Melchior. You'll make an outstanding Worshipful Master. This ring was practically made for you!"

The new Worshipful Master didn't respond to the compliments, he'd never liked being complimented.

To satisfy some of his uneasy feelings, Ben was determined to ask questions, "Mr. Tamworth, before we move on to whatever else is in your briefcase, how did your grandfather know I would ask about this place? How did he know I'd ever contact you or make an offer?"

Doug stared at Ben for a moment, "Ben, my grandfather knows you very well, perhaps even better than you know yourself. He's quite fond of you and to be honest so am I. Perhaps you can ask him more about that when you see him. He wants to come out here for a visit when his health improves."

Ben thought for a moment about Mr. James and how much he'd like to see his old friend again and thank him for all of this. The thought made him feel a little calmer.

The young man's thoughts were interrupted as Doug continued, "Ben, you should get over your displeasure of compliments. You deserve all of this and more. You are very worthy my friend!"

Doug paused as he wanted to let that sink in. He looked around and then returned his gaze to Ben, "You know, Ben, I think you were so intent on leaving Arkansas that you failed to realize how nice it is here. I've been here several times and spent most of my life just north in Kansas City. It's actually lovely. I can't imagine why you ever left. Here's to second chances young man, and I'm excited about what you'll accomplish here!"

Ben wanted to tell Doug how a person's perspective of a place could be tainted if they lived there in poverty, but Doug kept speaking.

"Ben, we're back to that one more thing I need to offer you before I go," Doug continued referring to the envelope he'd pulled from his briefcase and handed to Ben.

Ben opened the envelope and found a check inside.

"Please, Ben, accept this donation from James Tamworth to the Decatur Club for Boys and Girls to help get you started here. That should cover your operating expenses for a while," Doug said, smiling as Ben looked over the check and was clearly speechless.

"If you don't mind, Mr. Gilsum, I have to get on the road and head back to Kansas City," Doug said as he led them to the front door.

Ben followed slowly, silently, still staring at the check and unable to hold back his emotion. He breathed in a shaky breath and nearly began to cry. The young man regained enough of his composure to speak, managing to say just one last thing before Doug Tamworth got into his Lexus and drove away. "Please, Doug, tell your grandfather something for me as soon as you're able. Tell him I promise to trust myself and spend the rest of my life earning it."

Acknowledgments

Writing The Third King: Coronation started as little more than a whim. I'm not a literary scholar. I have no background in writing. I hope that wasn't too obvious in the preceding text. Imagine the confusion of my wife and children when the whim became a passion and the passion consumed all thought and conversation. Thank you to my wonderful wife Renee and my awesome children Emily and Austin for hanging in there with me and encouraging me all the way to the finish line.

Thank you to my parents who both passed years before I had the crazy idea to write a book. They're here, all over the pages. My mother encouraged me and made me feel like I was on to literary greatness with every sentence. My father didn't say much, but his pride and admiration was abundantly obvious. We both knew it. He didn't need the words.

Thank you to my brothers and sisters who put up with me, the youngest and clearly most handsome, beloved Campbell. I'm sorry Ben is an only child. It's nothing personal. A special thanks to my sisters Rhonda and Julie for all you did to support me during the process.

Thank you to Steve Hobbs, author of Retreads and New Hope, and his fabulous wife Jennifer for taking me through the first few baby steps of the process and showing the world of support out there for aspiring authors. Your willingness to answer questions and give encouragement made me want to be just like you when it's my turn.

Thank you Susan Baracco, editor, ghostwriter, book coach, author, and creator of Story Architect for Women. I'm so grateful that you agreed to collaborate with me and edit The Third King: Coronation. I'll never forget the moment, during our final video conference, when you made be believe

I was an author. Thank you for making my story better and making me better.

To Dennis Kouba, The Editing and Proofreading Guy: Thank you for putting the final polish on the project. Also a special thank you for reminding me to look down once or twice while walking down King Street.

Jay Sennott is a longtime family friend and very talented artist. I would like to say thank you for designing a beautiful cover. Not bad for a couple of guys who had never done any of this before.

Finally, to the fabulous cast of characters who exist in my life: Thank you. You're all in here somewhere, in some form, with a different name. I truly appreciate you all.

About the Author: Brian D. Campbell

Brian D. Campbell lives in Goffstown, NH with his wife Renee and their two children Emily and Austin. The Business Studies graduate of Southern New Hampshire University began writing The Third King: Coronation unsure if he would ever complete it. After falling in love with the characters and their story, Brian is proud to have completed this remarkable freshman offering and he hopes you'll enjoy this first installment of The Third King series.

Made in the USA
Middletown, DE
20 January 2019